Tag's stomach d— [wicked smile]

Oh yeah, he thought. No doubt about it, she had a smile capable of rendering a grown man stupid. The outfit didn't hurt, either.

Or lack of outfit.

Did she have any idea how she looked standing there in the glow of the lamp wearing a sheer black creation with wispy little straps? His tongue tingled to nudge those straps off her shoulders.

This was bad, very bad. It wasn't often he found himself speechless, but when she stepped closer words escaped him. Unable to stop himself, he reached out to slip a finger beneath her strap, urging it down. He felt her warm, soft skin, felt her breath catch.

Almost unaware, he dipped his head to hers. He didn't have far to bend. She was tall, which he'd just discovered was an incredible turn-on. Lying down, they'd be chest to chest, thigh to thigh, and everything in between would line up so damn perfectly....

She tilted her head so that now they were mouth to mouth, breathing each other's air, which was the most erotic thing he'd ever experienced.

She licked her lips and they were so close he felt the brush of her tongue against his lips.

"Mmm," she whispered. "It's a night for this, don't you think? A night for a hot, wet kiss."

Blaze™

Dear Reader,

My first Blaze novel has finally arrived! I have to admit, I wasn't sure I could pull it off, writing an extra, *extra* sensuous love story. But from the very first word of *Naughty But Nice*, this story wrote itself. It flowed so fast and hot I singed my fingers on a daily basis writing...ahem, shall we say *certain* scenes?

For that alone, I will forever have a soft spot in my heart for the bad girl Cassie Tremaine and the even badder Sheriff Sean "Tag" Taggart.

I hope you enjoy reading their story as much as I enjoyed writing it. And don't forget to pick up my good friend Leslie Kelly's BARE ESSENTIALS book, *Naturally Naughty*, also available this month. Look for my new Temptation series, SOUTH VILLAGE SINGLES, starting in January 2003!

Happy reading!

Jill Shalvis

P.S. I love to hear form readers! You can reach me through my Web site www.jillshalvis.com or by writing me at P.O. Box 3945, Truckee, CA 96160-3945.

Books by Jill Shalvis

NAUGHTY BUT NICE

Jill Shalvis

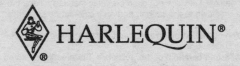

HARLEQUIN®

TORONTO • NEW YORK • LONDON
AMSTERDAM • PARIS • SYDNEY • HAMBURG
STOCKHOLM • ATHENS • TOKYO • MILAN • MADRID
PRAGUE • WARSAW • BUDAPEST • AUCKLAND

To Wanda,
You held my hand on this one, and I'll never forget it.

And to Birgit Davis-Todd,
For always being there when I needed you.

Thanks, ladies, and here's to many more....

ISBN 0-373-79067-8

NAUGHTY BUT NICE

Copyright © 2002 by Jill Shalvis.

This edition published by arrangement with Harlequin Books S.A.

® and TM are trademarks of the publisher. Trademarks indicated with ® are registered in the United States Patent and Trademark Office, the Canadian Trade Marks Office and in other countries.

Visit us at www.eHarlequin.com

Printed in U.S.A.

Prologue

Ten Years Ago

THE LINE OF CARS heading out of the Daisy Inn was long but giddy. After all, it was prom night. The night of hopes and dreams. The night of spiked punch and lost virginity. The culmination of high school, where one was to have the time of one's life.

Unless you were a Tremaine, of course.

In the town of Pleasantville, Ohio, the only thing worse than being a member of that family was being a *female* member.

Cassie Tremaine Montgomery, an extremely female Tremaine, looked over at her date. Biff Walters. Hard to imagine any mother disliking her newborn son enough to name him Biff. But his name had nothing to do with the reason why Cassie had agreed to go to the prom with the tall, blond, gorgeous—but stupid—football star.

No, the reason had everything to do with his graduation present from his daddy—a cherry-red Corvette.

Since Cassie had a love affair with all things expensive and out of her reach, the convertible had been irresistible.

"Hey, baby," Biff said, catching her eye and putting his big, beefy, sweaty paw of a hand on her thigh. "You look hot tonight."

How original. *Not.* So she was blond and five foot ten, with the stacked body of a *Playboy* model—she'd been that way since the age of thirteen. Which meant men had been drooling over her for four years now. Added to that was the fact that while the men in her family were bastards—some quite literally—the women were all tramps. No exceptions. There was a rumor it even said so in the law books.

She could live with the stigma, or get the hell out of Pleasantville. The town didn't care much either way.

Unfortunately as a kid, the second option had never been viable. She and her cousin Kate had grown up learning that lesson all too well. Cassie's mother, Flo, otherwise known as the town vixen, had long ago guaranteed her daughter's fate by cheerfully seducing as many of the husbands in town as possible.

By default, Cassie was as unpopular—or popular if you asked the men—as her mother.

Which burned her; it always had. So Flo had a weakness. Men. So what? Everyone had a weakness. At least her mother's was basically harmless.

"Wanna go to the lake?" Biff asked hopefully.

Ugh. The lake was the typical make-out spot just outside of town. Tonight it'd be crowded with over-eager guys toting their dressed-to-the-hilt dates, if they were lucky enough to have coaxed them out there.

Not for her, thank you very much. Cassie didn't share her mother's weakness for men, and never would.

"Of course you want to go, you're a Tremaine." Biff laughed uproariously at that. His fingers squeezed her thigh and moved upward, leaving a damp streak on the designer silk dress she'd secretly purchased at a thrift store.

"All the Tremaine women love sex." He was confident on this. "The wilder the better. It's why I asked you to the prom. Come on, show me what you've got, baby." Leaning over, he planted his mouth on the side of her neck, smearing beer breath over her skin.

Smiling when she wanted to puke, Cassie backed away and combed her fingers through the hairstyle she'd spent hours copying from an ad in *Cosmo*. Fine price she was going to pay for wanting a cruise through town in a hot car. Now she had to figure a way out of the rest of the night. "What's the rush?"

"This." Biff, panting now, put his hand on his erection to adjust himself.

Oh, good God, men were ridiculous. The smell of beer and sweat permeated the car's close quarters. "Biff, they didn't let us buy beer before the prom, remember? We got carded."

"I know." He looked extremely proud of himself.

"So why do I smell it on you?"

His grin was wide, wicked and stupid. "Jeff had a twelve-pack in the bathroom. He gave me half."

Six beers. Cassie wasn't afraid of much, and God knows the town thought her a brainless drunk in the making simply because of the misfortune of her genes but, contrary to popular belief, she was very fond of living. "You drank them all?"

"Yeah." They pulled out of the inn in a show-off peel of tires. The car swerved, making Cassie grab the dashboard with a gasp.

"Don't worry, baby." He sent her another ridiculously dumb grin. "I drive better under the influence."

Right. Damn it, graduation was only a week away. Freedom loomed like a rainbow over her future. Seven days and she was outta this one-horse town and she wasn't going to ever look back. She was going to show the world she could be someone. Someone special.

But she had to be alive to do it. "Biff, pull over."

"Now, baby—"

"Stop the car," she said through her teeth. If he called her baby one more time she was going to scream. And then she was going to make *him* scream.

"Watch this." He stomped on the gas and whipped into the oncoming traffic's lane to pass a slower car. "Woo-hoo!" He craned his neck to look backward, flipping his middle finger at the driver as he came back into the right-hand lane with one second to spare before causing a head-on collision. "Bitchin'!"

"Biff." Cassie's fingernails, the ones she'd so carefully painted candy-apple red, dug into his dash. "I—"

"Ah, shit," he said at the same time Cassie heard the whoop of a siren. Flashing lights lit up Biff's face as he swore the air blue.

They pulled over. When Cassie saw Sheriff Richard Taggart coming toward them, all she could think was *Thank God*. He'd just saved her from a car accident. Or at the very least, a wrestling match with an idiot.

Biff was still swearing, and Cassie couldn't blame him. The sheriff wasn't exactly a warm, fuzzy sort, though she did trust him despite his being a tough hard-ass. She trusted him because he was the only man she knew who hadn't slept with her mother, and therefore the only man she knew worthy of her respect.

He came to the driver's window. Tipped his hat back. Switched his gum from one side to the other. Calmly and quietly assessed the situation with his sharp, sharp eyes. "You kids heading anywhere special?"

"Are you kidding? Look at my date." Biff leaned back so the sheriff could see Cassie. "I got me a Tremaine for the night."

The sheriff looked at Cassie. Something in his eyes shifted. "The lake, huh?" he asked.

Biff just shot his idiotic grin.

The sheriff shook his head. "Get out of the car, Biff."

"But Uncle Rich—"

"Out of the car," the sheriff repeated. "You won't be driving again any time soon. I can smell you from here."

"Ah, man—" Biff started to whine, but sucked it up when the sheriff glared at him.

"Start walking home, little nephew. Before I arrest you for Driving Under the Influence."

Biff slammed out of the car like a petulant child and without so much as a backward glance at Cassie, whose panties he'd wanted to get into only five minutes before, started walking.

Fine. Cassie tossed her hair out of her face and did her best impression of someone who didn't care what happened. But her heart was pounding, because though she was grateful he'd pulled them over, suddenly she felt...nervous.

That was ridiculous. He was rough and edgy, ruled the town with an iron fist, but he was also fair. A pillar of the community.

No reason for her to feel anxious. After all, what would he do now? He'd probably just make her walk home, too. Yeah, that worked for her. The entire evening had been a bust anyway. She had no idea why she'd thought dressing up and going out with the most popular jerk—er, *jock*—would be fun.

"Cassie."

"Sheriff."

"Don't you dress up nice."

He was staring at…her breasts? That didn't seem right. Cassie managed to keep her shock to herself. "I—yes."

"You think the dress changes what you are?" he asked softly. "Or who you are?" His gaze ran over the black silk, which had been designed to make men beg for mercy. She'd loved it when she'd found it, she'd loved it all the way until this very second, but now she felt like hugging herself.

"Get out of the car."

She didn't move, and he leaned in. "I can make you," he said silkily. "In fact, I'd like that."

There was no one around. Not that anyone would have stood up for her if there had been. No doubt the people in the cars driving by figured she'd done something to warrant the sheriff pulling her over. Chin high, Cassie got out of the car. Casually leaned back against it. Tossed her head. Played cool as a cucumber. "What can I do for you, Sheriff?"

"What can you do for me?" He stepped close. So close she could see the lights from his squad car dancing in his eyes. Smell his breath. Feel his hips brush hers. She wanted to cringe back, wanted to panic, but no way in hell was anyone in this goddamned town ever going to see her panic.

"What you can do for me, Cassie, is rather complicated, though being Flo's daughter…"

"You…know Flo?"

"Intimately."

He was aroused. And he had been with her mother. Odd how that felt like such a betrayal. But she was very careful not to react because it was one thing to mess with a stupid eighteen-year-old punk driving his brand-new car. It was another thing entirely to mess with a fully grown, aroused man with a badge. Fear threatened to paralyze her but she tossed her hair back again. "You must have mistaken me for my mother then."

"I don't make mistakes." He lifted a hand.

It hovered in the air between them for a long moment, while Cassie held her breath. When she released it, his fingers danced along the very tops of her breasts, which were pushed up and out by her dress. His breathing changed then, quickened, and she realized he was no different from his nephew at all. The knowledge that any man, even this one, could be turned into a slave by his own penis was disturbing.

Skin crawling, she slapped his hand away. "Unless you're going to arrest me for having the poor judgment to go out with your idiot nephew, our business here is over," she said with remarkable calm. "Get out of my way. I'm walking home."

"I can give you a ride. Maybe Flo is home. Maybe the two of you would be interested…"

She shivered at the obvious innuendo. He wanted the both of them together. And why not, right? After all, a Tremaine was a Tremaine.

How did her mother stand this? Seducing men at the drop of a hat because she could? Cassie understood Flo enjoyed the power of bringing a man to his knees with lust, but Cassie would rather bring a man to his knees with pain. A direct kick to the family jewels would do it.

But this wasn't the man to do that to. Keeping her smile in place, she pushed past him. "Sorry, Sheriff. Not in the mood tonight."

Her heels clicked on the asphalt as she started walking. *Don't follow me, don't follow me.* She felt him watching her every step of the way, until she turned the corner.

Only then, when she knew she was truly alone and out of his sight, did she break stride and start running. No one stopped her. No one cared enough to.

Down Magnolia Avenue to Petunia Avenue, and then finally she turned off onto Pansy Lane. For the first time she didn't stop to sneer at the ridiculous flower names of the streets, and instead ran down the driveway of the duplex she'd shared all her life with her mother.

Her aunt and cousin lived on the other side. Kate would be a huge comfort right now, the voice of calm reason, but she'd still be with her date from the prom. Probably having the time of her life.

Cassie didn't go inside the house. Didn't want to face her mother, who would get misty-eyed at the sight of Cassie all over again. They both knew Cassie was leaving, and soon. The day she graduated, if possible. She had a life to find.

And someday she'd come back here and show them

all. She'd come back driving a fancy car. She'd live in the biggest house on Lilac Hill, just because she could. And…oh, yes, this was her favorite…she'd get the sheriff. Somehow, some way.

But most of all, she'd…become someone. Someone special.

She went around the side of the duplex to the backyard. Kicked off the Nine West pumps she'd saved all last month for and dug her toes into the grass. Tipping back her head, she gauged the distance she had to jump in the dress wrapped around her like Saran wrap.

And took a flying leap for the rope ladder. In her skimpy black dress, she shimmied up the tree and landed in the tree house that had served as her and Kate's getaway all their lives.

It was cramped. And musty. Probably full of spiders. It'd been a long time since she'd needed to be alone, but she needed that now. Desperately. She was close—far too close—to losing it, when losing it was not an option. Ever.

Opening the small wooden cigar box she and Kate kept hidden, she took out her private and personal vice and lit it. A cigarette. It helped steady her nerves. There was also her diary, and Kate's, inside the box. She reached for hers.

Leaning back against the trunk of the tree, she studied the stars, mentally reviewing the list of things she wanted to accomplish with her life before she scribbled them into her diary. Kate would get a kick out of the fancy-car goal, she was sure of it.

When she was done writing, she leaned back and watched a falling star, and though she would have denied it to her dying day, she wished.

She wished that life would get better soon as she got the hell out of Pleasantville.

1

Ten Years Later

SHERIFF SEAN TAGGART—Tag, as he was commonly known—had eaten, showered and was sprawled naked and exhausted across his bed when the phone rang.

"Forget it," he muttered, not bothering to lift his head. He didn't have the energy. God, he needed sleep. He'd been up all night helping a neighboring county sheriff chase down a man wanted for two bank robberies. Then this morning, before he could so much as think about sleep, he'd had to rescue four stupid cows from the middle of the highway. He'd also wrestled a drunken and equally stupid teenager out of a deep gorge.

Then he'd delivered a baby when the mother had decided labor pains were just gas so that she'd ended up stranding herself thirty-five miles from nowhere.

Now, though it was barely the dinner hour, he just might never move again. He lived alone on a hill above town. Not on Lilac Hill like the rich, but in a nice, comfortable, sleepy little subdivision where the houses were far apart and old enough to be full of character—aka run-down. His place was more run-down than most, which was how he'd afforded it.

Renovation had come slow and costly, so much so that he'd only gotten to his bedroom and kitchen thus far. But it was his, and it was home. After growing up with a father who ruled not only the town with an iron fist but his kid as well, and no mother from the time she'd left for greener pastures when he'd turned eight, having a warm, cozy home had become very important to him.

Truth be known, he was ready for more than just a home these days. It wasn't his family he wanted more of, as he and his father had never been close. How could they be when they didn't share the same ideas, morals or beliefs, and to the older Taggart, Tag was little more than a disappointment. Regardless of the strained relationship with his father, Tag felt he was missing something else. He was ready for a friend, a lover, a wife. A soul mate. Someone *he* could depend on for a change, instead of the other way around.

But right now, he'd settle for eight hours of sleep in a row.

The phone kept ringing. Turning his head he pried one eye open and looked at it. It could be anyone. It could be his father, ex-sheriff, now retired, calling to tell Tag how to do his job. Again.

Or it could be an emergency, because if life had

taught Tag any lesson at all, it was that just about anything could happen.

"Damn it." He yanked up the receiver. *"What?"*

"Dispatch," Annie reported in her perpetually cheerful voice. Off duty she was his ex-fiancée and pest extraordinaire. On duty, she was still his ex-fiancée and pest extraordinaire. Not long after becoming engaged, they'd decided they were better co-workers than co-habitors, and they'd been right. Tag could never have taken her eternal cheerfulness in bed night after night.

"Heard you didn't even kiss Sheila good night after your date," she said. "I'll have you know I went to a lot of trouble to set that up. You've got to kiss 'em, Tag, or you're going to ruin your bad-boy rep."

He groaned and rolled over. "God, I hope so."

"I just want you happy. Like I am."

She was getting married next month to one of his deputies, which was a good thing. But now she wanted him as almost married as she was. Sighing would do no good. Neither would ignoring her—she was more ruthless than a pit bull terrier. "If it's any of your business, which it's not, I didn't kiss Sheila because it wasn't a date. I didn't even want to go in the first place—" Why was he bothering? She wouldn't listen. Rubbing his eyes, he stared at the ceiling. "Why are you calling?"

"Know why you're so grumpy? You need to get laid once in a while. Look—" As if departing a state secret, she lowered her voice. "Sex is a really great stress reliever. I'd give you some to remind you, just as a favor, mind you, but I'm a committed woman now.''

Tag wished he was deep asleep. ''Tell me you're not calling me from the dispatch phone to say this to me.''

''Someone has to, Tag, honey.''

''I'm going back to sleep now.''

''You can't.''

''Why not?'' He heard the rustling of papers as Annie shifted things on her desk. He pictured the mess—the stacks, the unfiled reports, the mugs of coffee and chocolate candy wrappers strewn over everything—and got all the more tense. ''Look at the computer screen in front of you,'' he instructed. ''Read me your last call.''

''Oh, yeah!'' She laughed. ''Can't believe I forgot there for a moment. There's a stranger downtown, driving some sort of hot rod, causing trouble. We've received calls on and off all day, complaining about the loud music and reckless driving.''

He opened his mouth to ask what had taken her so long to say so, but bit back the comment because it wouldn't do him any good. Back on duty whether he liked it or not, he rubbed his gritty, tired eyes and grabbed for his pants. ''Theft? Injuries?''

''Nope, nothing like that. Just the music and speeding.''

''Speeding?'' He'd given up sleep for speeding? ''Why didn't...hell, who's on duty right now...Tim?

Why didn't he take care of this earlier if it's been a problem all day?''

"Seems Tim stopped off at his momma's for some pie after lunch and got sick. Food poisoning. He's been bowing to the porcelain god ever since. Poor guy, bad things like that don't usually happen here in Pleasantville.''

Since he'd had plenty of bad things happen to him right here in this town, the least of which was caving in and hiring his ex on dispatch, Tag just rolled his eyes. "If nothing really bad could happen, why can't I manage a night with some sleep in it?''

"Because we all love your sweet demeanor too much. Now get your ass up. Oh, and careful out there, okay? Don't do anything I wouldn't.''

Which was damn little and they both knew it. "Yeah, thanks,'' he muttered, looking for more clothes. He jammed on his boots, yanked on his uniform shirt and grabbed his badge.

With one last fond look toward his big, rumpled, very comfortable bed, he shook his head and left.

Halfway to downtown Pleasantville, his radio squawked. "Got the license plate and make for ya,'' Annie said, and rattled it off.

"Sunshine-yellow Porsche.'' Tag shook his head at the idiotic tourist who'd probably taken a wrong turn somewhere and ended up in Pleasantville. "Shouldn't be hard to find. Owner's name?''

"Let's see, it's here somewhere…Cassie Tremaine Montgomery.''

Not a tourist. Not a wayward traveler lost by accident. Not by a long shot.

Cassie Tremaine Montgomery.

She'd belonged here once. Though now, as a famous lingerie model, she was as far from Pleasantville as one could get.

He might not have ever met her personally since he'd been several years ahead of her in school, but her reputation preceded her. A reputation she'd gotten—according to legend—by using men just like her mother.

If he remembered correctly, and he was certain he did, Cassie had been tough, unreachable, attitude-ridden and…hot. Very hot.

And she'd been practically run out of town after her high school graduation by rumors. They'd said she was pregnant, on drugs, a thief. You name it, someone in town had claimed she'd done it. Hell, even his loser cousin Biff had plenty of wild stories, though Tag had no idea how much of it was true given Biff's tendency toward exaggeration. He'd never expended any energy thinking about it.

But now he was sheriff and she was back, stirring up trouble. Seemed he'd need to think about her plenty.

He saw her immediately, speeding down Magnolia Avenue in her racy car, with a matching racy attitude written all over her. Blond hair whipping behind her, her fingers tapping in beat to the music she had blaring.

Knowing only that things were about to get interesting, Tag turned his cruiser around and went after her.

GET WHAT YOU CAN, honey. Get what you can and get out.

Cassie Tremaine Montgomery smiled grimly as she remembered her mother's advice on life and took Magnolia Avenue at a slightly elevated speed than was strictly allowed by law. She couldn't help it, her car seemed to have the same attitude about being in this town as she did.

In other words, neither of them liked it.

As she drove downtown throughout the day, running errands, people stopped, stared. Pointed.

Logically, she knew it was the car. But the place had slammed her into the past. People recognized her. People remembered her.

Had she thought they wouldn't? Hadn't Kate warned her after she had been back in town recently to close up her mother's house? Good old Pea-ville.

There was Mrs. McIntyre coming out of the Tea Room. The Town Gossip hadn't changed; she still wore her hair in a bun wrapped so tight her eyes narrowed, and that infamous scowl. She'd maliciously talked about Cassie and Flo on a daily basis.

But that was a lifetime ago. To prove it, Cassie waved.

Mrs. McIntyre shook her finger at her and turned

to a blue-haired old biddy next to her. That woman shook her finger at Cassie, too.

Well. Welcome home. Cassie squashed the urge to show them a finger of her own. She couldn't help it, this place brought out the worst in her.

But she wasn't here to reminisce and socialize. God, no. If left up to her, she'd have never come back. There was nothing for her here, nothing.

Kate was gone. She'd marched out of town hand in hand with Cassie all those years ago, each determined to make something of themselves.

Kate had done spectacularly in Chicago, with her specialty ladies' shop, Bare Essentials.

Some would say so had Cassie. But that she could afford to buy and sell this sorry-ass town was little satisfaction when just driving through made her feel young and stupid all over again. Two things she hadn't felt in a very long time.

Everyone in Pleasantville had assumed she'd grow up the same as the trouble-loving Flo. Destiny, they'd said. Can't fight it.

And if you counted going off to New York and becoming one of the world's most well-known lingerie models following her destiny, well then, that's what Cassie had done.

Now she was back. Not by choice, mind you. Oh, no. She passed the library. And yep, there was the librarian standing out front changing the sign for tonight's reading circle. Mrs. Wilkens hadn't changed a bit, either. She was still old, still had her glasses around her neck on a chain and...was still frowning at Cassie.

Cassie had spent hours at the library looking for an escape from her life, devouring every historical romance novel she could find.

Mrs. Wilkens had always, always, hovered over her as if she was certain Cassie was going to steal a book.

Oh, wasn't this a fun stroll down memory lane. With a grim smile, Cassie drove on. She passed the old bowling alley, the five-and-dime, the Rose Café.

Pleasantville had a scent she'd never forgotten. It smelled like broken dreams and fear.

Or maybe that was just her imagination.

There was sound, as well. Other cars, a kid's laughter...the whoop of a siren—

What the hell? Craning her neck in surprise, she looked into the rearview mirror and saw the police lights. Her heart lurched for the poor sucker about to get a ticket. A serious lead-foot herself, Cassie winced in sympathy and slowed so the squad car could go around her.

It didn't.

No problem, she'd just pull over to give it more room. But the police car pulled over, too.

And that's when it hit her. *She* was the sucker about to get the ticket.

"Damn it. *Damn it,*" she muttered as she turned off the car and fumbled for her purse. She hadn't been pulled over since...prom night.

All those unhappy memories flooded back, nearly

choking her. She hadn't given thought to that night in far too long to let it hit her like a sucker punch now, but that's exactly what it did. Her drunken date. Then dealing with the sheriff, who'd been one of the few men in town she'd figured she could trust.

She'd been wrong, very wrong. No man was trustworthy, hadn't she learned that the hard way? Especially recently.

But after all the terror she'd been through in the days before she'd been forced back here, Cassie wasn't going to get stressed about this. She'd find her wallet, explain why she was in such a hurry, and maybe, just maybe, if she batted the lashes just right, added a do-me smile and tossed back her hair in a certain way, she'd get out of here ticket-free.

Please, oh please, let there have been a new sheriff in the past ten years, she thought as she finally located her wallet in the oversize purse that carried everything including her still-secret vice—a historical romance. Pirates, rogues, Vikings…the lustier the better. She hadn't yet cracked the spine on this latest book, but if the sheriff saw it she'd…well, she'd have to kill him.

"Damn it."

No driver's license in the wallet. Oh, boy. Her own fault, though. In getting ready for the club she'd gone to several nights ago with friends, she'd pulled out her license and stuck it in her pocket so she wouldn't be hampered by her heavy purse.

And she hadn't returned it, not then, and not in the shocking events since. "Damn it."

"You said that already."

Lurching up, Cassie smacked her head on the sun visor, dislodging her sunglasses. Narrowing her eyes at the low, very male laugh, she focused in on...not Sheriff Richard Taggart, thank God.

No, Richard Taggart would be in his late fifties by now. Probably gray with a paunch and a mean-looking mouth from all the glowering he'd done.

The man standing in front of her wearing mirrored sunglasses and a uniform wasn't old, wasn't gray and certainly didn't have a paunch. In fact, as her eyes traveled up, up, up his very long, very mouthwatering body, she doubted he had a single ounce of fat on his tall, lean, superbly conditioned form.

Not that she was noticing. She worked with men all the time. Fellow models, photographers, directors...and while she definitely liked to look, and sometimes even liked to touch—on her terms thank you very much—this man would never interest her.

He wore a cop's uniform and a sheriff's badge, and ever since prom night she had a serious aversion to both.

Not to mention her aversion to authority period. "I don't have my license," she said, dismissing him by not looking into his face. Rude, yes, but it was nothing personal. She might have even told him so, if she cared what he thought, which she didn't.

"No license," he repeated.

What a voice. Each word sent a zing of awareness tingling through her every nerve ending. He could have made a fortune as a voice talent. His low, slightly rough tone easily conjured up erotic fantasies out of thin air.

"That's a problem, the no-license thing," he said. Having clearly decided she was no threat, he removed his sunglasses, stuck them in his shirt pocket and leaned on her car with casual ease, his big body far too close and…male.

She took back the whole voice-talent thing; he should go bigger and hit the big screen. She didn't need her vivid imagination to picture him up there as a romantic action-adventure hero.

Without the uniform, of course.

Obviously unaware of the direction her thoughts had taken, he nodded agreeably at her lack of inclination to apologize over not having a license. But one look at that firm mouth, hard jaw and unforgiving gaze, and Cassie knew this man was agreeable only when it suited him.

A car raced past them, a blue sedan with a little old lady behind the wheel. "Hey," Cassie said, straightening and craning her neck to catch the car vanish around the corner. "That lady was going way faster than me!"

"Mrs. Spelling?" He shrugged and tapped his pen on his ticket book. "She's late picking up her grandkids."

"She's *speeding,*" Cassie said through clenched teeth.

"Well, you were speeding first." He cocked his head all friendly-like. "And you're not carrying your ID because…?"

Because she'd left New York in a hurry. That was what happened when three incredibly shocking things occurred all at the same time.

One, she was being stalked. The man doing so had been a friend. That is, until she'd declined to sleep with him—which is when it'd turned ugly. Seems that if he couldn't have her, he wanted her dead.

Her agent, her friends and her fiercely worried cousin had all insisted she get the hell out of Dodge— and since Cassie was rather fond of living, she had agreed. What better place to disappear than in a town that had never seen her in the first place?

Two, her mother had decided to sail around the world with her latest boyfriend. She would be away indefinitely, which meant she'd left Cassie a surprising and early inheritance. That Cassie had been forced to come back to Pleasantville to take care of that inheritance coincided with her need to vacate New York for a while.

The third shocking thing wasn't life-altering, but had bothered her enough that she'd dreamed of it for the past several days. Kate had found their high school diaries and the ridiculous lists they'd each made that fateful night in the tree house after their disastrous prom. Lists that included their childish wish for revenge on a town that had always spurned them. Cassie's was inspired, if a bit immature, and she eyed the sheriff again, remembering what she'd written.

1. Drive a fancy car, preferably sunshine-yellow because that's a good color for me.
2. Get the sheriff—somehow, some way, but make it good.
3. Live in the biggest house on Lilac Hill.
4. Open a porn shop—Kate's idea, but it's a good one.
5. Become someone. Note: this should have been number one.

Amusing. Childish. And damn tempting, given that she had already nailed number one. Maybe that's all she'd ever accomplish, driving a fancy yellow car, but one thing she'd come to realize in her most interesting career, she had a zest for life.

She wanted to live.

But if anyone thought she wanted to live *here*, they needed to think again. She'd rather have an impacted wisdom tooth removed. Without drugs.

She took off her sunglasses and immediately wished she hadn't. The glare of the sun made her squint, and she hated to squint. She also felt…exposed. The way she hadn't felt since her very first day of kindergarten, walking in with a big smile that slowly faded when all the other kids and their mean moms had stopped to whisper.

Tremaine.

White trash.

Daughter of a tramp.

Wild child.

At age five, she'd had no idea what those whispered words meant. But even then she'd recognized the judgment, so she'd simply lifted her chin to take the verbal knocks. She did the same now. "I don't have my license because it's not in my purse," she said, refusing to explain herself to anyone in this town. Including a cop. Especially a cop.

"Hmm. I hadn't realized Cassie Tremaine Montgomery was famous enough to not need ID."

"You know who I am."

His lips curved. "I've seen the catalogs. Interesting work you've gotten for yourself."

"Those catalogs are for women."

"With you in silk and lace on page after page?" He shook his head, that small smile looking quite at home on his very generous mouth. "Don't fool yourself. Those catalogs are scoured from front to back by men all across the country."

"Is that why you pulled me over? You wanted to meet me in person?" Disdain came easily for any man with authority, especially this one. "Or is it because I'm driving an expensive and brightly colored sports car?"

"Contrary to popular belief," he said conversationally, "cops don't necessarily have an attraction to all cars painted red or yellow. What we do have, however, is an attraction to speeding vehicles.''

"And this has to do with me because...?"

"Because you were speeding," he said in that patient—and incredible—voice that told her he thought she was the village idiot, not the other way around. Then he straightened and waved his ticket book. "The question now is, were you going fast enough to warrant reckless driving."

Cassie never gaped, it went against the grain, but she did so now. "You've got to be kidding me."

As he had before, he leaned in, resting his weight on his arm, which lay across her open window. It wasn't a beefy arm, or a scrawny one, but somewhere in between, more on the side of tough and sinewy.

Again, not that she was noticing. He was probably a jackass, as Richard Taggart had been. He was probably prejudiced against anything different from his small-town norm. He was probably mean-spirited and stupid, as well—most men that good-looking were. For the second time she considered going the batting-the-eyelashes route. It would work. She'd been rendering men stupid with her looks for a very long time now.

In that spirit, she put her saucy smile in place to butter him up. His slate-blue eyes went as sharp as stone. He wasn't going to fall for the saucy smile, damn it, so she let it fade. "Look, I wasn't reckless driving. And you already know who I am so the license isn't really necessary."

In front of them, an older couple started to cross

the street. Cassie ignored them until they stopped and stared at her, then started whispering furiously to themselves. Recognition came sharply to Cassie— they'd run the drugstore years ago, where she'd done her best to prove to the town she was just as wild as they thought by purchasing condoms regularly. "Oh, forget it," she said on a sigh. "Just do what you have to do."

"Which would be what, do you think?"

Well, hopefully it wouldn't be to make her get out of the car so he could try to feel her up. "You could let me go."

He smiled at that. A slow, wide smile that had her heart skipping a beat. "But you were speeding."

"Maybe I'm in a hurry to get out of here."

"Wouldn't be the first time, so I hear."

Now what would he know about her fast exit after graduation? She took another long look at him, squinting through the bright sun to see his name. *Taggart*. Oh, my God. "You're…"

"Sheriff Sean Taggart. You can call me Tag, most do."

Suddenly she could hardly breathe. She couldn't have managed a smile to save her life. Pulling back, she stared straight ahead out her windshield. "You're Richard's son."

"That would be correct."

It wasn't bad enough she'd had to put her entire life on hold because some jerk had decided if he couldn't have her, he'd terrorize her. Or that she had to be here while her life was on hold. No, she had to run into her old nightmares to boot. That, added to her current nightmares... God, she needed a cigarette.

Too bad she'd quit smoking five years ago. ''Just give me my ticket then.''

He was silent for so long she broke her own code and turned to look at him. Silent—still, even—but not idle. His eyes reflected all sorts of interesting things, mostly curiosity. ''You know my father.''

No. Her mother had known him. Cassie had just hated and feared him. ''The ticket?''

''Now you're in a hurry to get your ticket? What's up, Cassie?''

The sound of her first name in his incredibly sensuous voice seemed so...intimate. ''Like I said, I'm in a hurry to get out of here.''

''Are you on your way out then? Already?''

She opened her mouth to remind him that was none of his business but her cell phone rang. It was Kate.

''Did you get there yet?'' came her worried voice across the line. ''Are you okay? How is it? You run into anyone we know? Talk to me.''

Cassie stared up at the tall, dark and intensely handsome sheriff. ''Kate, your timing is something.''

''Oh, honey. Who is it? That mean old Mrs. McIntyre? Mrs. Wilkens? Because if it is—''

''As a matter of fact,'' Cassie said, slowly smiling as her and Tag's gazes locked. ''It's Sheriff Taggart.''

''Is that old fart still sheriff?''

''No, Tag here is Richard's son.'' When her gaze ran down the front of him, slowly, across his broad shoulders and what looked like a very promising chest and flat belly, over his trousers, which lovingly cupped powerful thighs and everything in between, then back up again, he lifted a daring brow, then gave her the same slow perusal.

Good, she thought in triumph. He *was* just a man after all, a man run by the equipment between his legs. A man who'd possibly forget to write that ticket due to the fact her little yellow sundress not only matched the car she'd bought herself last year but also accented the body she'd been well paid for over the years.

"Cassie," Kate said into her ear. "I worry about you there, all alone."

"I'm used to being alone." Funny how that worked. She was surrounded by people all day long and yet it was true. She was utterly alone.

"I mean because of your stalker."

Cassie's stomach tightened with the fear she pretended not to feel and glanced at Tag, who was unabashedly eavesdropping. "I'm safe enough here." *She hoped.*

"The guy slashed all your tires in the hopes of leaving you stranded, remember?"

"I do."

"And then he ruined two photo shoots—"

"I remember all of it, Kate."

"I'm sorry, of course you do. Okay, subject change. You going to be okay facing what Flo left you?"

That had been a shocker. That her mother had actually come out on the winning side after all, after always being considered the town joke. Seems the men in her life had come through, over the years gifting her a prime piece of real estate downtown, an amazing turn-of-the-century house on Lilac Hill overlooking town, and supposedly some other equally valuable things she needed Cassie to take care of. Cassie still couldn't believe it.

"Cassie?"

"I'm okay, Mom," she said, and accomplished what she'd wanted. Kate laughed.

"Call me back."

"Oh, I will." She clicked off and tossed the phone into the back seat. Then looked at Tag. "So…"

Tag looked right back. "What do you mean, you're safe enough here?"

"It's considered rude to eavesdrop."

"Talk to me, Cassie."

Oh, *right*. Terrified as she might be in the deep dark of night, she'd rather face the boogeyman bare-ass naked before asking this man for help. "If I do, can we skip the ticket?"

Now he laughed and, good Lord, she hoped that wasn't a weapon he used often because just the sound could make a grown woman quiver with delight. She was fighting doing just that—uniform or not—when he flipped open the ticket book and started writing.

2

TAG ACTUALLY MANAGED a night of uninterrupted sleep, mostly due to the fact that he'd turned off the ringer on his phone and had shoved his pager beneath the couch pillows.

Not being on call did wonders for his mental health. What hadn't done wonders for that same mental health had been his dreams.

X-rated dreams about Pleasantville's latest visitor. He doubted they'd sprung from the photographs in the lingerie catalog he'd received in the mail and had perused over dinner. Photographs that showed every perfect inch of the body that belonged to one Cassie Tremaine Montgomery.

Lord, she was stacked. All long, tanned…lush. With the wild mane of sun-kissed blond hair and come-hither mouth…man, she was sure built like a goddess.

A tempting goddess, for certain. But luckily, not his type. A woman like Cassie was trouble, and on top of that trouble, he imagined she'd be high maintenance.

Tag was done with high maintenance, done with

people needing him to take care of every little thing. The next time he let a woman into his life—and there would be a next time—it was going to be for keeps. She was going to be a sweet, quiet little thing who lived for him.

Yeah. *He* was going to be the high maintenance one for a change.

But as he showered, it wasn't the quiet little woman that came into his mind. It was Cassie. As in his dream, her cynically lit eyes were hot with passion, her mouth wet from kissing him, and her amazing body wrapped around his. Not only wrapped, but soft and pliant and so ready for him she would explode when he plunged into her.

Now *there* was an image to make a shower nice and steamy and his body hard and achy. Nothing he couldn't take care of by himself. But that wasn't what he was looking for.

Once the hot water turned cold, Tag got out, slipped on his uniform pants, and reluctantly put Cassie out of his mind. Even more reluctantly, he pulled his pager from beneath the couch cushions.

His father had called—again. He'd probably heard about the tri-county arrest, the one in which it had taken the authorities—including Tag—three days to apprehend the suspect. Yeah, ex-sheriff Richard Taggart probably wanted to make sure Tag knew *he* would have done it in one day.

Well, hell. So he wasn't like his father. So he didn't believe he had to bully the town into obeying the law.

Hallelujah. But it'd be nice if just once, just one damn time, his father could acknowledge Tag's success.

Tag ran a hand through his wet hair and bit back a sigh as he strode through his very quiet house to the kitchen, where he poured himself a bowl of cereal.

"Note to self," he said to no one in particular. "The little wife will make me a hot breakfast every morning."

Soon as he found her.

The phone rang. Not surprisingly, it was Annie.

"Hey, boss, get your sweet ass up. We're short-staffed. Turns out Tim didn't have food poisoning, it was the flu, and half the staff is out."

"Any bright yellow Porsches out there speeding this morning?" he asked.

"Just one."

And he was just in the mood for it, too. He slipped into his uniform shirt, grabbed his badge and hit the road.

He found her immediately, cruising downtown, rolling through a four-way stop where he'd cleaned up more accidents than he liked to remember. Pulling her over, he strode up to the driver's side of her car and had to laugh at the look of fury on her beautiful face.

"Let me guess," Cassie said through her teeth. "You haven't met your ticket quota yet for the week."

"Careful, or I'll think you like me." He grinned when she snarled. "Did I mention yesterday that the speed limit is enforced here? As well as the *full stop* sign, which by the way, means you're supposed to come to a full stop. It's a ticket if you don't.''

She rolled her eyes and tapped her red-lacquered-tipped fingers on the wheel, the picture of impatience. ''I'm in a bit of a hurry.''

''You know, you'd get farther with honey than vinegar,'' he said, pulling out his ticket book.

''I save the honey for someone who'll appreciate it.''

Well, she had him there. She could bat her pretty lashes and flirt all she wanted, he was pretty much fed up with the tactic. No way could she bowl him over with those sexy green eyes and walk away. Nope, he was far tougher than that.

Maybe he wasn't big city. Maybe he had only the badge and his training behind him, but he was his own man and he knew what he wanted.

And okay, he wanted her. He was red-blooded, after all. But a quick affair to let off some steam wasn't enough for him, not these days. Slumming around no longer appealed. He wanted for keeps. The real deal.

Nothing about Cassie was the real deal.

''Meow.''

This came from the passenger seat, on which sat the biggest, fattest tabby he'd ever seen. ''Well, hello,'' he said, and when the cat climbed all over Cassie to get to him, obviously using nails for leverage if Cassie's hiss was any indication, he obliged it by reaching in and scratching beneath the chin.

A loud rumble filled the car.

Cassie narrowed her eyes at the purring cat. "Look at that, the Daughter of Satan likes men. What a surprise."

"Daughter of Satan?"

She sighed. "Sheriff, meet Miss Priss. Miss Priss meet—" She glared at the cat when it growled at her. "Oh, never mind, you're so huffy and snooty and rude you don't deserve an introduction."

"Funny," Tag said. "I would have said the same thing about her owner."

"I don't own this cat, and I'm never huffy. Snooty and rude, most definitely. But not huffy."

Despite the fact he didn't want to acknowledge his dreams hadn't been as good as seeing her in the flesh, his gaze gobbled her up. She was wearing white today. White tank top, white mini skirt, white leather boots. It seemed almost sacrilegious, all that virginal color on that mouth-watering body. *Down, boy.* "Why doesn't your cat like you?"

"It's not my cat, it's my mother's. Apparently they frown on felines on cruise ships, so she left the thing for me to take care of, along with—" She sent him a look designed to wither. "Why am I telling you all this?"

"Because I'm irresistible?"

For one moment she let her guard down and laughed. Her entire face softened, and he stared at her in shock. My God, she was beautiful like that, he thought, and wondered what it would be like to see her happy, really happy.

But then he took back the thought. He didn't care what she looked like happy; he'd prefer to see what she looked like from the back, heading right out of town. "Let me guess...you're on your way out of here."

Now her frown was back, on those perfectly glossed lips. "I wish." She flipped her hair out of her eyes and lifted a shoulder. "I think you might be stuck with me a little bit longer. Hope you can handle it."

"The question is, can your car insurance handle it." He opened his ticket book and she sputtered, making him laugh again. "Why do I get the feeling that not many have crossed you?"

"Why do I get the feeling you don't care?" she muttered.

When he'd handed her the second ticket in as many days, she grabbed it, tossed it over her shoulder into the back of her car and took off, her hair flying in the wind, her cat back in the passenger seat. The two of them were frowning, two obnoxious females thrusting their chins out against the world.

HONEY, do what you got to do. The blazes with anyone else. Cassie heard Flo's voice in her head clear as day. More rarely she heard Edie's voice, Kate's mother, and for all intents and purposes Cassie's

Mom No. 2. It seemed Cassie's bold-as-brass lifestyle leaned more toward Flo's advice than Edie's.

She wondered if hearing voices meant she was going crazy, or just that Pleasantville was getting to her. Both, she decided, and stripped out of her clothes, fingering through the things she'd brought, looking for some comfy pajamas.

She was a clothes hound and, thanks to her job, had collected many beautiful things. They were a comfort to her, the silk and lace, and proved, if only to herself, she was no longer poor.

Poor had meant longing, yearning, helplessness, and she hated all three. She would never long, yearn or be helpless again.

She thought of her little stalking problem—the slashed tires, her ransacked apartment, the threatening letters—and shivered.

Well, *hopefully,* she'd never feel helpless again.

In her suitcase she came across a tin of cookies her agent had given her. Cookies were a rare treat for a lingerie model, but since she'd canceled work for the entire summer, she tore into them and grabbed her book.

The Savage Groom. Maybe some good old-fashioned French Revolution period lust would clear her head. At least she could afford her books now instead of sneaking into the library and past the haughty Mrs. Wilkens for them.

''Chocolate,'' she moaned out loud and stuffed another in her mouth. Happy and cozy in imported silk, a fattening cookie in one hand and a book in the other, she flopped back on the bed and let herself relax for the first time in too long. "Two days, two tickets and a pounding headache. That's got to be some kind of record, even for me."

Another weight hit the bed and Cassie lifted her head. Her gaze collided with the slanted yellow one of Miss Priss. "You."

"Meow."

Cassie tried to shoo her off, but the cat wasn't only annoying, she refused to budge, letting out that terrible wail she had.

"Meow."

"Hey, I just fed you…" When had that been? "Yesterday." Oh, man, good thing she wasn't a mother. Just as she opened her mouth to apologize, the cat turned in a circle, presented her behind and sat within an inch of Cassie's nose.

"Eww, *move.*"

Miss Priss did. She moved closer and, claiming half the pillow with her big, fat, furry body, she began to clean herself. Her private self.

"I am *not* sharing a pillow with someone who licks her own genitalia."

Miss Priss didn't seem to agree, and with a bolt of ingenuity, Cassie grabbed the spare pillow and threw it at the cat, who landed with a hiss on the floor. Leaning over the edge, she smiled smugly. "Stay."

"Mew."

That was an "I'm sorry" mew if she ever heard

one. Damn it. What was she doing, snapping at a cat? Wasn't that like kicking a puppy? With a regretful sigh, she reached out a peace offering in the form of a cookie, and—

"Ouch!" Yanking back her scratched palm, Cassie sat up. "That's it. Go play on the freeway."

"Mew."

"Oh, fine." She got up and fed the ingrate. Then, using both pillows now, she settled back on the bed against the headboard.

The sound of a roaring truck ruined her peace, and she went to the window. The trash truck. Now there was a job. The guy on the back of the truck hopped off at her neighbor's house and hoisted the cans. He had a slouch and a gut and...and it was Biff. In an instinctive gesture she backed from the window. Assessed how she felt.

And grinned. There had to be some justice in the world if she—a Tremaine—was living on Lilac Hill and Biff—former star football player—was collecting her trash.

She called Kate, who'd appreciate the irony.

"Kate, Biff is the trash guy," she said when her cousin picked up the phone. "And he's not even the driver. He picks up the trash."

"Perfect job for him, I'd say."

Oh, yeah, she could count on Kate. "I'm sprawled on the most luxuriously silk-covered bed in a luxurious bedroom surrounded by the most amazing, luxurious house. Can you believe it? My mother lived like a queen after I was gone.'' And because it felt good, so good to relax, she arched her neck.

"My God," Cassie murmured.

"What? A spider?"

She stared at herself in the mirror framed above the bed. She'd seen the mirrors before now, of course, but they were still a shock. She studied herself dispassionately. Her body was barely covered in azure-blue imported silk, showing off her full breasts and the belly that didn't look quite as flat as it should for a lingerie model. With a grimace, she tossed the cookies aside. "No, it's just this place. The garage is full of furniture from the duplex and my mother has mirrored ceilings."

Kate let out a startled laugh. "Well, we always knew Flo wasn't a prude."

Funny how even though Cassie knew exactly who and what Flo was—a woman unable to resist a man, any man at all—when it came right down to it, it was hard to picture her own mother having sex on this bed and enjoying the view from above. "You realize I'm on Lilac Hill, right? *Lilac Hill*. My fancy neighbors would have a coronary at the secrets this bedroom holds."

"I imagine that was part of the fun for her."

Ever the voice of reason, her Kate. Despite Kate's own demons, she'd always helped Cassie see things differently. And more importantly, she made Cassie smile. "Flo did enjoy a good scandal. But Lilac Hill, for God's sake." The place that as children they'd stared at enviously, fantasized over. "I feel like I fell down the rabbit hole."

"You deserve it," Kate said with a sudden fierceness in her voice. "Both of you. You've worked so hard all your lives, and now Flo is sailing the Greek Islands and you're a world-famous lingerie model. You both paid your dues for so many years. You're supposed to enjoy this."

"But I miss work." Cassie sighed. "The photo shoot I bailed on this week was in the Bahamas."

"Which is where your stalker was going to meet you. Isn't that what the last threat said?"

Yes, but she didn't want to go there. She *so* didn't want to go there. "So I'm here. In a house my mother never paid for."

"Of course she did. She loved…who was it—Mr. Miller the banker, right?—and he cared enough about her to give it to her. Just like Mr. McIntyre, who left her that building downtown." She laughed. "I bet Mrs. McIntyre is spitting nails over that."

"Oh, yeah. If looks could kill, I'd be six feet under. Which reminds me." Cassie took a deep breath. "I have some ideas." She sat up because she had to be careful how she phrased this. After all, Kate was a Tremaine, which meant that like Cassie, she had more pride than sense when it came to accepting help. "You said you were ready to open another shop."

"I said I *wanted* to open another shop, I never said I *would* open another shop. Successful as I've been in Chicago, I don't have the money for that yet."

"I know. But I do."

"I'm not taking any more of your money. I just paid back the start-up loan you gave me for the first Bare Essentials."

"I'm not talking *money,* per se. I want you to take the building, the old men's store that Flo inherited from horny old McIntyre."

"No."

"Kate."

"Cassie."

Cassie had to laugh at Kate's calm annoyance. "Stop it. I have an ulterior motive."

"If you want a new toy, all you have to do is ask. We just stocked up."

"Hey, I still have Mr. Pink that you bought me for Christmas and I just loaded up on batteries, thank you very much."

Miss Priss leapt back onto the bed, and with one long daring glare, she settled at Cassie's head.

"If I wake up with a fur ball lodged in my throat, you're dead meat," Cassie told the snooty cat. "And you," she said to her cousin, "will you listen to me for a moment?"

"You got one minute. Fifty-nine, fifty-eight, fifty-seven…you'd better hurry."

"Should have been a comic, Kate. Listen, I want you to have the building because it feels right. I don't know what to do with it, and it's just sitting there going to waste. Besides, it's right downtown. Right smack in the middle of downtown…are you following me here?''

"Let me see if I am…you see Bare Essentials, basically a very naughty ladies' store—"

"One which sells a most excellent dildo, I might add."

"Thank you. You see Bare Essentials fitting right in with the Rose Café and the five-and-dime."

"Why not? This town could use some spice."

"More than having their wild child come home?"

"Hey, they made me this way. Come on, say yes. It's on our lists of things to do…"

"Cassie." Kate laughed. "Those lists were written by bitter teenagers."

"So?"

"So…it's not that easy. I was just there, I don't want to move back to that place any more than you want to be there."

Cassie flopped back on the bed and stared at herself in the ceiling mirror. Her agent had cleared her schedule for the entire summer and it was only early June. The police and her friends had convinced her that a low profile would be best.

She knew that to be true. No matter her outwardly brave facade and joking, cynical manner, she hated the fear, the terror. Because of it, she sat in Pleasantville with no one but a mean old cat for company and nothing to do but pay her moving violations.

Oh, and stare at the sheriff's ass. It was a mighty

fine ass, but that simply wasn't enough. Especially since he wasn't so much as slightly interested in her.

How long had it been since a man hadn't fallen in a pool of saliva at her feet? Didn't matter; unlike her mother, she had no need for a man to fall all over her.

"Cassie?"

"I'll get the shop going for you," she said rashly. "Come on, Kate. Opening a porn shop in Pleasantville. It doesn't get better than that."

"Bare Essentials, which is doing exceptionally well by the way, is *not* a porn shop." Kate sniffed.

"I know that. But everyone here will think it is." Glee leapt wildly within her. This idea just got better and better the more she thought about it. "This is inspired, truly inspired. I can keep myself from going crazy and—"

"Oh, honey. You *are* going crazy, I knew it. Maybe I should come back—"

"—and I can shock this mean-spirited old town while doing it. Mrs. McIntyre. Mrs. Wilkens. All of them. No, don't you dare come back. Unless of course, you want to. I can do this. I want to do this."

"Are you sure?"

"Absolutely. I can't just sit here and hide, Kate. I just can't. Otherwise every shadow, every little thing, makes me jump."

"Have you informed the sheriff about why you're really there?"

"Of course not. I'm fine. I just need to do something and this is perfect. What do you say?"

"You can't just give me the building. If we do this, it's as a team. And, damn, revenge on that godforsaken town sounds really good. Too good."

Cassie knew she had her. And if she did so in part because Kate was worried about her, then she was willing to play that card, because though she'd eat a stick before admitting it, she was worried about herself, too. "So then...?"

"Yes," Kate said. "Yes, let's do it. Partners?"

"Partners," Cassie vowed.

ONE WEEK—and another ticket—later, Cassie was still jerking awake at night, certain her stalker had found her. Just last night she'd opened her mouth to scream at the weight holding her down, only to find Miss Priss sitting on her chest. The cat she could handle.

She had also handled the town—by snubbing her nose every morning at her fellow shop owners on Magnolia Street. Specifically, anyone and everyone going in and out of the Tea Room right next door, most of the waitresses at the Rose Café, and anyone else who stopped to point and whisper.

This didn't include the Downtown Deli across the street, mostly because the deli was new, and therefore the legend of Cassie Tremaine didn't live there. And also because Cassie had discovered a weakness for pastrami on rye, along with the thirtysomething own-

ers Diane and Will. Silly Diane and Will, they actually seemed to like her.

Cassie's building had been cleared of old debris
and cleaned. They still had to paint, refloor and decorate, but that was the fun part. Since she was the one
in town at the moment, she would handle most of that,
happily. She loved to decorate and organize, and
loved to paint. Which was a good thing, as Kate was
notoriously bad at it, and was never offered a paint-
brush.

She and Kate had spent hours teleconferencing
over the stock for the store, with Kate sending
naughty sample after naughty sample. The UPS girl,
a very cute little thing named Daisy—only in Pleasantville—had continuously asked what was in all the
boxes she kept delivering. When Cassie had finally
broken down and told her—Daisy was simply too
sweet for both this town and its gossip mill—Daisy
had nearly swallowed her tongue.

In spite of it all, or maybe because of it, Cassie felt
like a little girl at Christmas. One night, during a
wicked early summer storm, she sat in the deserted
building, surrounded by boxes and Miss Priss.

The cat hadn't relented—she still hated Cassie—
but she refused to be left home alone. If Cassie did
leave her at the house, she paid for the mistake dearly
as Miss Priss wasn't above leaving "deposits" to
show her annoyance. Yesterday it had been in her
slipper, which Cassie had unfortunately put her foot

into, so she'd caved like a cheap suitcase and took the damn cat wherever she went.

Rain beat against the windows of the building, while thunder and lightning beat the sky. She'd lost power about thirty minutes ago, but undeterred, she'd lit a lantern. In her mind's eye, she could *see* the store, envision the displays, the music, the lights— everything laid out the way she and Kate had planned—and the work was so therapeutic, she didn't want to stop. Unafraid—a nice change—she sat alone on the floor making copious notes to share with Kate during their next phone call.

Bare Essentials. Even the name was perfect, and she jotted a note to talk to Kate about what type of sign they should have made to hang out front. Every- one in town would assume the worst, of course, and to make sure she fulfilled those thoughts, the shop would carry a variety of items for shock value alone. Maybe they could create an interesting window dis- play with cock rings and anal plugs....

Time flew by as she opened boxes, spread the sam- ples out this way and that, made notes, even tried some things on.

Miss Priss had long ago fallen asleep in a box. Outside, beyond the shuttered windows, traffic had dribbled to nothing.

Cassie, wearing a simple, basic black camisole— the design was so exquisite, she absolutely loved it— was sitting on the floor with the last box. She pulled it close and opened it. Inside she found a note from

Kate. "Think the lovely patrons of Pleasantville will like these?"

Cassie grinned as she laid out a selection of body jewelry. She could see the looks now, especially when the Pea-ville matrons were confronted with nipple and clit rings.

Cassie herself had once had her belly button pierced, but it had gotten in the way of certain photo shoots so she'd let it grow in.

But a nipple ring...if she wasn't such a chicken when it came to pain she'd have the real thing. Since she never would, that left the clip-on variety. She opened up a package that held a pretty, delicate-looking silver hoop, slipped a spaghetti strap off one shoulder and bared a breast. With her fingers she plucked her nipple into a hard bead and applied the jewelry.

With a hiss, she let out a slow breath. It was a clamp of sort, but surprisingly, it didn't hurt at all. And looking down at herself, she had to smile. "What do you think, Miss Priss? Pretty hot, huh?"

"Does my vote count?"

With a scream, Cassie leapt up, instinctively reaching out for a weapon as she did. That she grabbed Big Red—her nickname for a twelve-inch long, three-inch thick, glow-in-the-dark red dildo—didn't matter. The sucker was heavy and she could wield it like a baseball bat no problem.

"Whoa, just me."

In the back of her mind she recognized that incredibly sexy voice.

Not her stalker.

Not a Joe Blow off the street.

But dangerous, none the less. And she was standing there in a camisole with her faux-pierced nipple hanging out. Keeping hold of Big Red with one hand, she used the other to cover her breast. "You."

"Me," the sheriff agreed, partially stepping out of the shadows into the meager light let off by the lantern so that she could see just his face. His sharp eyes scanned everything, including her, while his long, rangy body remained utterly still. "I thought this building was supposed to be empty and I saw the light. Had a few complaints."

"Let me guess. Mrs. McIntyre?"

"Among others."

"I'll bet. How did you get in?"

"You have a bum door. It's locked but not shut all the way."

"Look, the place is mine, no one in this bitter old town can say otherwise, so if you're thinking about giving me another ticket—"

"Another ticket." God, that voice of his. "Gotta tell you, Cassie, I wasn't thinking ticket when I first saw you." He shifted closer. "Have you done anything illegal lately?"

As he asked, his gaze ran leisurely over her, making her very aware of how she must look standing there holding a big, fat dildo and her own breast. "Uh…"

"Other than indecent exposure, that is?"

"Indecent?"

He cocked his head and looked her over good, his eyes eating her up. "Actually, that's a matter of opinion."

She could feel her other nipple tighten; she told herself she was cold. Which didn't explain why the silk between her legs suddenly felt as soft and incredible as a man's touch.

As he still stood in the shadows, she couldn't see what he wore, but she imagined him in his uniform, and it hardened her against him despite the fact that he looked good enough to eat.

But the expression in his eyes as he drank in her scrap of black wasn't a cop's look. It was a man's.

And something within her tingled. Lord, he was something, all rough-and-tumble ready. He'd make a nice diversion, wouldn't he? If he wasn't such a cop.

Go for it, honey, said Flo's voice in her head. *Get what you can and get out.*

Standing there, he was tall, dark and shockingly, overtly sexy. It wouldn't be hard to "go for it." But beneath that laid-back, easygoing facade, he was tough as nails, and she knew it.

She'd never been shy about her own sensuality, but unlike Flo, she refused to let it run her life. Flo couldn't resist a man.

And yet Flo had always brought men to their knees.

Cassie liked that part. But something told her the big, bad Tag wouldn't be easy to control. Bottom line— if she couldn't be in charge, she never dallied.

Never.

Still, the summer loomed long and empty in front of her. If nothing else, surely she could get him to take care of her tickets…

Grab everything they'll give you, Flo would say right now. *Grab it and walk away.*

Tag's hot, hot gaze ran down her body, making her stomach quiver, making her forget the tickets. His gaze settled on Big Red. "Cassie, what were you going to do with that thing?"

Just his voice made her thighs clench. "Big Red? Did you know he glows in the dark?"

He lifted a brow. "What else does he do?"

He can drive you crazy, she thought, and let out a wicked smile.

3

OH, YEAH, Tag thought. No doubt about it, Cassie Tremaine Montgomery had a smile capable of rendering a grown man stupid. The outfit didn't hurt, either.

Or lack of outfit.

Did she have any idea how she looked standing there in the glow of the lantern wearing...what the hell was that black thing anyway? It had wispy little straps that would be easy to nudge off with one fingertip, or a single touch of his tongue. One already hung off her arm. The bodice was sheer, except for the lace roses that strategically covered her nipples.

Or nipple, since the one was hidden from his view not by the lace flower but by Cassie's own fingers. The sheer black slid over her belly and ended very high on her hips, with just a scant little strip disappearing between her thighs, where he imagined it was held together with a few strategic snaps.

His teeth itched to see how quickly he could undo them.

Which was bad, very bad. Even worse, just seeing her fingers on her own bare breast was enough to turn his insides quivering. She was touching herself, had been touching herself when he'd walked in. She wore a nipple ring and was handling the biggest dildo he'd ever seen. If there was a man in the world strong enough to not be brought to his knees by that image, Tag wasn't him. "Cassie, what are you doing here, dressed like…that?"

"Haven't you heard?" She seemed utterly unconcerned by her near nudity. He had to admit, he'd never seen a more mouth-watering, luscious body in his life. Covering it should be a crime. And if he was to believe even one quarter of the stories he'd heard about her, she apparently didn't have a problem with *un*covering it.

"We're putting a new store in this building," she said.

"We?"

"My cousin Kate and I. Bare Essentials. It's a bit of a secret what we're selling."

"Why?"

"It's going to be a…ladies' shop."

"Ah. You want to shock the good people of Pleasantville."

"Oh, yeah, we do. You caught me playing with some of the merchandise." She hefted the dildo in her free hand. "Think the good ladies of Pleasantville will admit to needing one of these bad boys?" She ran the tip—the very large, red, bulbous tip—across her collarbone.

His heart nearly stopped.

Down her stomach.

Riveted, he stood there practically panting.

"Hmm." She pursed her glossed lips. "That reminds me." The dildo dipped below her belly button. "We'd better sell batteries, too, don't you think? I'd hate to force some shy thing into the hardware store with this bad boy."

It wasn't often Tag found himself speechless. Or with an uncontrollable erection while on duty. "Your strap. It's…" He held her gaze as she stepped closer. Unable to stop himself, he reached out to slip a finger beneath her fallen strap, slowly bringing it back up. The material dragged over the breast she was covering with her hand making her other nipple tighten all the more. Her breath caught at that, he heard it, and it caused his own to do the same. Beneath his fingers he felt her warm, soft skin. Almost unaware, he'd dipped his head to hers. He didn't have far to bend. She was a tall woman, which he'd just discovered was an incredible turn-on. Lying down, they'd be chest to chest, thigh to thigh, and everything in between would line up so damn perfectly….

She tilted her head slightly, too, and his jaw brushed her long hair. A silky strand clung to the slight stubble on his cheek, and he stilled to keep it there.

She moved again, lifting her head so that they were mouth to mouth, breathing each other's air, which turned out to be the most erotic thing he'd ever experienced.

She licked her lips, and they were so close he felt the brush of her tongue against his lips. "Mmm," she whispered. "It's a night for this, don't you think? A night for a memorable kiss."

With a groan, he parted his lips and slid them to hers. Hot. Wet. Heaven. She opened for him and as his tongue lightly caressed, she gave in with a hungry sound that sent his every rational thought skittering out the door. Because it was quiet and relatively dark, and because he couldn't think with her so close to him, he gave in to the hunger. Her lips parted farther and the kiss deepened into an explosive, frantic, lush mating of mouths and tongues. And for one glorious moment they connected—lost, wild, clinging—until she shifted a fraction to stare at him with eyes satisfyingly full of hunger and passion.

He still had his fingers entwined in her camisole. Beneath them her skin felt like silk. Hot silk. The taste of her was still on his tongue—forbidden passion and the promise of head-banging, toe-curling sex. No doubt, he had to get her covered before this got out of control, but the material of her lingerie stuck to the hand she held over her breast.

Slowly, still holding his gaze prisoner in her own, she pulled her hand free, giving him a devastatingly thorough glimpse of that silver hoop on her puckered nipple. Utterly unable to help himself, he lifted his hand and ran the pad of a finger over the mouth-watering tip. The hoop danced, her breast quivered. And every bit of saliva in his mouth dried up. In that moment he knew he was out of control, that at the slightest invitation from Cassie, they would be naked and rolling on the floor.

Then she let the material cover her breast, and he managed to take a breath.

"Thanks," she whispered.

He would have whispered something back but he was still facing that whole speechless problem. Both nipples were hard, clearly defined. The one he'd just covered now had the clear outline of a circle around it, and picturing her placing that ring on herself all over again, he groaned.

"It's not real," she said softly. "It's just a clip-on. I was just—"

"Trying on the merchandise. I know."

"I have more. We have one for a guy." She ran a finger down his chest, past his belly to the top button of his pants, which she toyed with, making his already straining erection painful. "Want to try it on? I can do it for you. You put it—"

"*Cassie.*"

She actually smiled. "Chicken?"

"No." He let out a careful breath and caught her wandering fingers in his. "But I am on the very edge. Tease me another second and I'll prove it to you."

"Maybe next time, then."

"Yeah." His knees were actually knocking. Shocked at how much he wanted her, when she wasn't what he wanted at all, he pulled away, closer to the lantern. He needed to see things clearly, damn it, he needed the electricity back on. The dark was lending an intimacy to this little episode that he didn't need. He opened his mouth to say his goodbyes, maybe even offer an apology for barging in on her, for giving in to temptation, but Cassie had backed away, too.

No longer were her eyes open and warm. No longer was her body loose and relaxed. Instead she stood there staring at him as if he was the lowest form of life.

"What?" he asked, his head still spinning from their kiss.

She pointed at him with the dildo. "You're on duty."

Hadn't he already said so?

"I...hadn't really realized...you're in uniform."

Confused, he glanced down at himself. "Usually, this shirt is a turn-on for women," he said, thinking to tease because he was at a loss to understand her.

Not that he wanted to. No, what he wanted...well, *that* was as dangerous as understanding her.

"I'm not your usual woman," she said.

Wasn't that the truth.

"I'm not turned on by bad attitude and authority."

"Bad attitude?" He had to laugh. "I thought that was you."

Wrapping her arms around herself, she turned away, but not before he caught a quick glimpse of her own confusion. Her own pain. It stopped him in his tracks. But then he caught more than that. He caught a good look at the back of her, and nearly had heart failure.

There *was* no back to her outfit. It dipped down in an open scoop far past her waist, so low that if she so much as shifted he was going to get quite the view. There the outfit would have resembled a pair of hot shorts, except the words "hot shorts" were too conservative. In any case, the scant material divided the most delicious-looking butt cheeks he'd ever seen.

"You've done your civil duty," she said in a voice as cold as the south pole, which was in such direct opposition to that hot body he could only stand there gaping like an idiot.

"I'm not breaking and entering," she said. "I'm not speeding. There's really no need for you to be here."

Well, that much was true. As a cop he had no need to be there. But he glanced at his watch and was rewarded by the time. "I'm off duty."

She peered at him over one creamy shoulder and he lifted his wrist to show her. "It's five minutes past midnight, which was when my shift ended."

"A cop is always a cop."

Why was she so angry? Risking life and limb he came close again, reaching out to touch her cheek. "I'm just a man." A man who would die for another kiss.

She shifted away. "A *cop*."

Her skin had been warm. Soft. And he wanted more, but she was still backing away. He snagged her hand, knowing she was far too proud to look weak and to try to pull free. "I don't take my work home with me, Cassie. When I'm standing here with you like this, I'm not working."

She let out a laugh he was sure she meant to be harsh, but it came out more as a question, making her seem...vulnerable.

But why? Why was she wary of him? Was it him as a man or as a cop? Either way, his gut clenched.

She wasn't as tough as she wanted to be, and that was a huge shock. He thought he'd had her pegged; knowing he might be wrong about her was more than a little unsettling. Knowing that this hard-as-nails, gorgeous woman could be vulnerable did bad things to his resolution to stay away from her. With a little tug, he brought her closer still. Now he could smell her, all warm and clean and sexy female. His body went to war with his mind. His mind wanted to know more about her. Not his body; no, that part of him just wanted to haul her close. "Someone in a uniform hurt you," he guessed.

She lifted a shoulder, neither denying nor confirming, and a part of him actually ached. "I'm sorry," he said, and found himself startled to realize he meant it.

She lifted that shoulder again. "Don't be *too* sorry, Sheriff." She lifted the red dildo. "I was going to tease the hell out of you with this bad boy."

He stared at it, felt his mouth go dry again as his

penis jerked to hopeful attention. "You could still try."

The smile on her lips didn't meet her eyes. "Nah. The fun's gone." She stared pointedly at his hand on hers until he let go. "Good night, Sheriff."

"Good night, Cassie."

She waited until he got to the door. "You might think of me tonight," she said softly. "I'm taking Big Red home, along with a pack of batteries."

He groaned, and in tune to her low, satisfied laugh, he let himself out.

TWO WEEKS AFTER her arrival, Cassie was still keeping herself busy. She was in charge of readying the store, while Kate handled the inventory, getting lots of beautiful, sexy lingerie from her business partner and designer Armand.

Cassie made more calls to Kate, did more cleaning and painting. There was more delivering by Daisy in her UPS outfit and sweet smile.

It should be illegal to be sweet and innocent in Pleasantville.

Cassie had the Bare Essentials sign made, and the day it went up was fun. It gave her great satisfaction to stand directly beneath it and pretend she didn't see the commotion it caused.

Up and down Magnolia Avenue, which had been designed for pleasant foot walking, people came out of the woodwork and stared.

"They're talking," Daisy whispered. "About... you."

"Always." Cassie looked at her. "I'm sure you've heard the stories."

"Well, sure. You're a legend."

Cassie laughed. "A legend, huh?"

"No, really. You're a homegrown hero come back to her roots. You made something of yourself."

"I made *something,* all right." But Daisy didn't smile, and Cassie had to wonder...was she just imagining all the malicious curiosity? Her gaze met Mr. Miller's widow from across the street, where she stood just outside the deli. *Frowning.*

Nope, definitely not imagining it. But...she did have to admit, most of the negative energy was coming from the older generation.

Maybe that was simply because Cassie hadn't been around long enough to taint the younger one.

Since no one dared ask, she put up another sign, this one in the window, saying they'd open for business in two weeks.

"Two weeks?" Still wearing her apron, Diane came out from the Downtown Deli and stood under the sign. "Cool. I'm not sure what you're selling, but I have a feeling Will's going to love it."

Cassie stared at her as Diane simply smiled and walked away. But then she shook it off. She had work to do.

Two weeks in which to get the place ready to go. It would be a challenge for both her and Kate, but they were up for that. For Cassie, she needed something to keep her mind off her career, off the trouble that had brought her here.

Off the sheriff.

Because really, who would have thought such a man could melt bones with a simple kiss? A simple touch? But there had been nothing simple about either his kiss or his touch. She'd underestimated him, that was certain, and it wouldn't happen again.

Unless it was on her terms, of course.

Those terms were simple. If she could keep the control, if she could drive him crazy and walk away, then perfect.

Otherwise, she wasn't interested.

Time to get back to work. *Work.* Not really a decent description for what she'd been doing because she'd actually been enjoying herself, all the way down to dressing the part of a co-owner of a ladies' shop. She'd pulled out all the stops in that department, wearing some of the more outrageous clothes she'd collected over the years.

Take today, for instance. Her halter top had nothing but three straps across her back and her leather pants looked as if they'd been spray-painted on. After all, everyone expected the daughter of Flo to look a certain way—why not give it to them?

"Excuse me."

"Yes?" Cassie turned around on the sidewalk and faced a woman. She was dressed simply in jeans and a sleeveless blouse, little to no makeup, and looked to be around thirty. There was a two-year-old clinging to her hand. "Can I help you?"

"Are you going to sell…" The woman blushed a little, and bit her lower lip.

Cassie sighed. "Let me make this easy for you. Bare Essentials will be a fully stocked women's store. If you're embarrassed to ask for it, chances are good that we'll carry it."

The woman nodded, then laughed at herself. "I'm sorry. My name is Stacie Harrison. I've been wanting to introduce myself."

Probably wanted to satisfy her curiosity about the new harlot in town. Behind Stacie, literally hanging out of the Tea Room, were Mrs. McIntyre and her sister Mrs. Hampton. Their mouths were turned down in disapproving frowns. Cassie lifted a hand and waggled her fingers at them.

"Well, I never," one exclaimed.

"Really? You never?" Stacie tsked. "That's just a shame, ma'am."

Both of them let out a collective gasp and, with daggers in their gazes, vanished back inside.

Cassie turned and stared at Stacie, who giggled. "Are you insane? They're going to make you miserable now."

"No one can do that but me," Stacie said calmly.

Whatever. Stacie's social suicide was none of her business. Cassie had a shop to open. She was doing this, and people needed to just get used to it. Turning to enter her shop, she stopped when Stacie put a hand on her arm.

"Did you know we're neighbors? I live three doors down from you on the hill. I made you cookies last week but my ex-husband—the jerk—called and annoyed me, and I ended up eating them all myself. With Suzie here—" she smiled down at her toddler "—I haven't had a chance to make another batch."

"You...made me cookies."

"Yes." She smiled brightly. "My ex is a surgeon, you see. And he was boinking the X-ray tech. But the good news is I got the house."

Cassie let out a startled laugh.

"Anyway," Stacie went on, "I like to cook off my stress. I was going to bring them to you, maybe sit down with a glass of iced tea or something, and talk."

"I don't drink iced tea."

"Oh, well, that's okay." Stacie smiled. "Water would have worked."

What the hell was this woman's angle? "If you want to see the inside of Flo's house, all you have to do is ask. You know what? I'm thinking of conducting tours." She could make a fortune. Too bad it wasn't money she needed.

Stacie looked confused in the face of her sarcasm. "Flo? Who's Flo?"

Right. "You don't know my mother?"

"Should I?"

"She lived in the house before I did."

"Oh. I saw her a few times but I'm sorry to say I

didn't have the pleasure of meeting her. And…'' She looked around to make sure they were alone. "You know, I always wanted to live there, up on the hill, but to tell you the truth, now that I'm there I'm realizing it's awfully quiet. I'm going stir-crazy."

Uh-huh. The ex-wife of a surgeon. Mother of…a very sticky-looking kid. Bored? Cassie didn't believe it. Not in Pleasantville. No, the town she knew like the back of her own hand didn't breed nice, compassionate people. It bred smallness. Meanness.

And she was here to repay that in kind. "I've got to get busy."

"Sure. I'm hoping to bake again tonight. If I do, I'll stop by tomorrow."

"Uh-huh." Maybe Cassie should give tours of just the *bedroom,* show everyone the mirrored ceilings. *Wait.* Maybe they should *sell* mirrors to put on the ceilings!

"See you tomorrow then." Stacie smiled. "I'm glad we met."

Before Cassie could process the words, Stacie walked away, swinging her daughter's hand.

She was glad they'd met.

But how could that be?

CASSIE SPENT the rest of the day and the next readying the interior of the building. She'd been working on it all week, paying for manual labor when she had to, using high school seniors who were grateful for the cash.

And who didn't remember her from her youth.

She was sure their parents did, and wondered what they thought of Cassie now, paying their sons to do work for a Tremaine.

Then wondered why she cared. She *didn't* care. Not one little bit.

Oh, damn them all anyway. It burned like hell that she'd never accomplish that last thing on her list. In this town's eyes, no matter what, she'd never become *someone*.

And it burned even more that she thought about it.

It angered her enough to forego the cheap labor for the day and to do it all herself. The boys seemed quite disappointed when she'd told them to go. Cassie wasn't sure if that was because of the cash she paid them, or her overalls, under which she wore a comfy, but very skimpy, crop-top.

Didn't matter. They were gone and she was alone. Contrary to popular belief, she was very capable of hard work. She loved hard work.

The alone part was a little unnerving since she wasn't exactly here in town for a picnic. But surely she was safe.

She really wanted to think so. She *had* to think so.

She stood on a ladder, paint splattered across the front of her designer cargo overalls, enjoying the paint fumes, when her cell phone rang. She unclipped it from her belt and let out a happy smile at the Caller ID. "Kate, my love, you should see this delicious shade of pink I found. It simply screams 'come in, you must buy a new sex toy.'"

"I'd love to see it. How does next Friday sound?"

Cassie's grin widened. "You're coming!"

"I'm coming," she agreed, but with a surprising lack of enthusiasm. "I can't miss the grand opening, now can I?"

Cassie set down her brush and backed down the ladder. "What's the matter?"

"Nothing."

"Kate."

"Can't a girl just call her favorite cousin?"

"I'm your only cousin. Spill it. Does it have anything to do with that guy you saw when you were here? The one you won't tell me about?"

"Jack? No."

"Then what?"

Across the miles, her cousin sighed. "You remember how before you left, you arranged to have all your mail forwarded to me for the duration?"

"Yes." Cassie's heart kicked into gear. "So no one could locate me through the postal service while I'm here. What's the matter, are my bills piling up?" Her mouth was suddenly dry. "You were going to just send them on to me, and—"

"It's not your bills."

"Too many magazines, huh?" *Oh, God.* Please don't let it be what she feared.

"It's not the magazines, either. Though I am enjoying *Playgirl*, thanks."

"Okay." Cassie pulled off the painter's cap and let her hair fall free. She sat on an unopened five-gallon can of paint and unhooked one side of her overalls for freedom of movement. "Let me guess..." She was surprised at how fast her pulse could race. "You got a letter from him."

"He's not happy you've vanished from the face of the earth, Cass. He's scaring me."

He was scaring her, too. *Peter*. One of the first men she'd met when she'd gone to New York. He was a photographer, and he'd taken her first publicity shots for a price she'd been able to afford—a date. They hadn't slept together because unlike Flo, Cassie had her own personal standards, which included never sleeping with a man when business was involved.

So they'd become casual friends. And as Cassie's career had boomed, she'd done her best to get Peter jobs. Occasionally, while between relationships, he'd drink too much and try to tell Cassie she was the one for him. She always gently turned him down, knowing his next girlfriend was right around the corner, and she'd always been right.

Their friendship had sustained.

Until now.

Now, he was her stalker.

Cassie shivered. Though she was not a woman to let fear run her life, this guy truly got to her. Enough to have uprooted everything.

Hard to admit she'd been stupid enough to actually trust a man. And look what it had gotten her. He'd taken her away from her career, away from her life, and sent her back to a town she was fairly certain wasn't ready for her. Wouldn't *ever* be ready for her.

"He says he's never going to stop looking for you, Cassie," came Kate's stressed voice. "You're the only one for him, and if he can't have you, he says no one else can, either."

Okay, now her heart was ricocheting off her ribs. She'd known he'd never really recovered from the last dumping by that waitress/actress-wannabe.

And this time, unlike the others, he couldn't seem to wrap his mind around the fact Cassie wasn't interested in him that way.

Not only not interested, but good and truly scared. He'd broken into her place. Touched her things. Left her a threatening note on her mirror in her own lipstick. *You're mine.*

Then he'd vanished. Which is why the police hadn't been able to get to him. Which was how she'd ended up with a restraining order, and then landed herself here. "I'm okay here, Kate. I never talked about my past with Pete."

"Are you sure?"

"What do you think?"

Her cousin actually let out a relieved little laugh. "Yeah. How silly. Thinking you'd open up and tell someone about yourself. Much less open up to a *man.*"

"He has no idea I'm not a native New Yorker.

Even all those years ago when I first got started, he had no idea.''

"Okay, but I'm still coming. I want to see you. It's been too long. And I want to do more to get the store ready—the opening will be a thrill. Can't miss that, or the chance for some good old-fashioned revenge. And then there's my mom's house. I have to take care of that situation. I talked to Flo and I'm going to stay in her half of the duplex, since Mom is renting out her side.''

"And you know all of Flo's old furniture is in my garage. We'll haul it out for you when you get here.''

"Which won't be until Friday so I'd feel better if you'd tell someone there what's going on.''

Cassie snorted. "Who am I going to tell, someone in the Tea Room?''

"How about the sheriff?''

"I'll see you soon, Kate.''

She sighed. "Love you, Cass.''

"Love you, too.'' Cassie clipped the cell phone back onto her belt and stared sightlessly across the future Bare Essentials. Kate was worried.

And damn it, so was she. Big time.

4

ON CASSIE'S WAY HOME that night she made a trip to the library. For nostalgia's sake, she told herself, moving directly to the small paperback section at the back. It smelled the same and, oddly comforted by that, Cassie sank into one of the beanbag chairs that had surely been in the same spot since the flower-power sixties. How many hours had she sat in here, inhaling one historical romance after another, lost in a world that had always been a better world than hers?

"Oh, Barry, stop. You're making my knees weak."

What? Cassie craned her neck. Behind her, in the doorway to the backrooms, stood Mrs. Wilkens whispering into a cell phone.

"I know you're my husband, you silly man. But I told you, we can't have phone sex until my break." She grinned.

The old lady with the severe white bun and pursed lips *grinned*. At her husband. As he gave her phone sex.

Cassie had entered the twilight zone.

"Call me later," Mrs. Wilkens whispered. "Yes, I'll bring home another romance novel, don't worry.

Some new ones just came in…. I love you, too." She slipped her cell phone into her pocket and then went very still when she saw Cassie.

Who didn't quite know what to say. A definite first. "You…you have *phone sex?*" she managed to say.

"Romance readers have a sixty percent better sex life than nonreaders," she sniffed. "If I'd known you were coming, I'd have put out some more books for you."

"You'd have…" Cassie narrowed her gaze, suddenly transported back in time. Every time she'd sneaked into the library, she'd always found a stack of new books seemingly waiting just for her. It had been her own little miracle. Her oasis in a life of hell. "You…" Oh, my God. *"You."*

Mrs. Wilkens nodded. "We had the same tastes. And it seemed to keep you off the streets."

"But…I thought you hated me."

Mrs. Wilkens smiled, her face softening. "You thought everyone hated you. Hang on, I'll find you some books."

Oh, yeah. She'd definitely entered the twilight zone. But Mrs. Wilkens came back with three books Cassie had been eager to read. Unbelievable.

When she finally left the library and drove home, she sat in her car for a moment, staring up at the big, dark house on Lilac Hill, wishing she'd thought to leave every light burning.

"Meow."

"Yeah, yeah." With one last apprehensive look at

the dark walkway, Cassie got out of the car, reached for the cat and got hissed at for her efforts. "Fine. Walk. Hope there aren't any dogs out here."

Miss Priss lifted her chin and leapt from the car like royalty, leading the way with her head held high.

Cassie had to admit, the attitude helped. When she imitated the cat and threw her shoulders back, head up, she felt better. Invisible. Or was that invincible?

She just wished she had claws like Miss Priss, on the off chance she needed them.

But no one jumped out and yelled boo.

There was, however, a package on the porch, which gave her one bad moment. She opened it, pretending her fingers weren't shaking as she did so, and found the most incredible-smelling batch of chocolate cookies. Her mouth watered—mostly because she'd skipped lunch.

"What do you think, Miss Priss? Poisonous? Or delicious?" When the cat didn't so much as look at her, Cassie took a tentative bite. "Mmm."

She'd been walking through the decadent house flipping on all the lights, munching on cookies for dinner, when the knock came at the door. Cassie opened it and found the woman from town standing there, minus the toddler.

"Hi, remember me? Stacie?" Stacie grinned at the cookie in each of Cassie's hands. "Oh, good. You're enjoying the goodies I made."

"They're heaven," Cassie admitted. "I have no

idea how I'll fit into my work clothes in the fall, but thanks.''

Stacie smiled. ''No problem.''

Cassie nodded in what she considered a friendly, neighborly manner, not that she'd ever had any neighbors to be friendly with. When she'd lived in this town growing up, she hadn't been allowed to talk to her neighbors—except for Kate—as in the house on one side of the duplex had lived a man who'd sold drugs, and in the other the resident had a police record a mile long.

In New York, she'd never even seen her neighbors.

So she didn't have a lot of experience to go on here. She waited for Stacie to get to the bottom of her visit. To tell her what she wanted.

But the woman just stood there. Cute as a button. Still smiling.

''Uh…'' Cassie offered a half smile. ''So…''

''This is where you invite me in for a drink,'' Stacie said helpfully.

''Oh.'' Cassie looked over her shoulder and wondered if she'd cleaned up after herself. ''Well…''

''That's okay.'' Stacie reached out and squeezed her hand. ''We can work our way up to that. But you could do me one little favor.''

Here it was.

''Tomorrow's opening day of the carnival.''

''Carnival.''

''Don't tell me you don't know about Pleasantville's annual carnival! The one to raise money for arts in the schools. Held at the beginning of every summer.''

Oh, Cassie knew all about the carnival. She'd sneaked her first beer at the carnival. Her first cigarette.

Lost her virginity.

Oh, yeah, she had a whole host of whoopee memories from the annual event. ''Let's just say I'm not particularly fond of it,'' she said carefully.

''Oh.''

Stacie looked so disappointed, Cassie sighed. ''What's the favor?''

''I'm going to be sitting in the dunking booth. Thought you'd come by and say hi. Since the divorce I haven't socialized very much and…'' She lifted a shoulder and let out a little laugh. ''And it's been a bit lonely, you know?''

Friends. Is that what Stacie wanted? Ha! Obviously she hadn't been listening to the town gossip lately. As for lonely…ah, hell. ''Yeah, fine. I'll stop by.''

Stacie's entire face lit up, and before Cassie could blink she was enveloped in a hug. ''See you tomorrow,'' Stacie whispered, and then she was gone.

Leaving Cassie with one more thing to think about.

PLEASANTVILLE'S ANNUAL carnival brought out the best and the worst in the general population. There were clowns, games, crafts, rides and enough junk food to keep the town in stomachaches for the rest of the year.

There were also whiny kids, grumpy parents, the occasional drunk and a slew of trouble-seeking high school kids out to score.

Not to mention the heat. Dark had fallen and yet at nearly ninety degrees, the temperature hadn't.

Not exactly the way Tag would have chosen to spend a Saturday night. He wasn't on duty, not officially anyway, but they were still short staffed due to the flu, and he knew his presence would help.

The music pulsed loud, as well as all the hooting and hollering from the rides and games. Pulling his shirt away from his damp skin, he strode up and down the aisles thinking of how he'd *rather* be spending his evening.

In front of ESPN. With air-conditioning.

No, scratch that. In the arms of a woman. Yeah, now there was a way to pass time. His nice, quiet, sweet, loving woman, whose entire life would center around him and his needs. And though she'd be quiet, she wouldn't be shy. No way. She'd be wildly passionate and erotically sensual.

She'd greet him at the door wearing his opened shirt and nothing else but a smile.

Now there was a fantasy.

He strode down a row of games, then around a corner to another aisle, stopping to gulp down a large lemonade. People had shown up in force tonight to support their schools, but few had found this area yet. He could see straight ahead to the dart game, where all one had to do was pop three balloons to win a prize.

A woman stood there. There were women all over the place, but this one, dressed to kill in her jade-green haltered sundress, stood out. She was concentrating fiercely, her back to him as she threw back her arm, aimed...and missed.

He knew that long, slim back. Those blond waves tumbling over straight, proud shoulders. Those long, long legs that could wrap around a man and—

"Shit," she muttered, and shoved a hand into her pocket. That she came out with another buck surprised him, as her skirt appeared to have been painted on.

Several women passed Cassie, each of whom stopped to stare at her, then kept going, laughing unkindly. Tag frowned and opened his mouth to say something but Cassie flipped them off and went back to shooting.

It made him grin.

And suddenly he was incredibly glad he'd come. Still grinning, he sauntered up to the booth and leaned a hip against it as he turned casually toward her.

She didn't even glance at him, just accepted her new darts from an awed-looking, pimply-faced teenage boy and aimed again.

Two balloons in a row, bull's-eye. Pop. Pop.

"One dart away for the big prize," the boy told her with a huge, dopey smile on his face. "You have to hit all three to get the—"

"I know what I have to do." She threw the dart.

"Close," Tag said conversationally when she missed by a mile. "But no cigar."

Oh, she noticed him now. Narrowed her very incredible, very green, very expressive eyes on him. "You distracted me."

He lifted his hands. "Hey, you didn't even see me until just now." Slipping a hand into his pocket, he came out with another buck. "But here. Try again, on me."

"I'm not taking your money." She slapped down her own dollar. "Back off, you're in my space."

"Backing off." But he didn't. She smelled too good, looked too good. He wasn't going anywhere.

She didn't even notice. In fact, she appeared to forget about him as she took aim. And this time hit her target. Then did it again.

"One more time," the kid said, ever so helpfully, and Cassie lowered the third dart and glared at him. He took a step back. "Sorry. I just know how bad you want this pretty teddy bear here."

"Teddy bear, huh?" Tag tucked his tongue into his cheek as she aimed and once again missed her third and winning shot. "I gotta tell you, I never really pictured you as a teddy bear type, Cassie."

"Oh, she wants it really bad," the kid offered as Cassie grated her teeth. "She's already put at least ten bucks on it."

"Is that right?" Tag looked at Cassie and lifted a

brow. "You need something cuddly to sleep with at night, Cassie?"

She sighed. "Is there a reason why you're standing there staring at me?"

"Well..." He scratched his jaw and looked her over, from the long neck he suddenly wanted to nibble on, to the breasts nicely outlined behind her halter, down her curved hips and mile-stretch legs. Her toenails were hot pink tonight, and she wore a silver toe ring, reminding him of the nipple ring. Was she wearing it now? "You are something to look at."

With a roll of her eyes, she slapped down another buck and went back to the task at hand. Aimed. Let it rip, and Tag had to admit, she knew what she was doing.

Pop. Pop.

Two balloons down.

"Only one to go," he offered.

Her hand lowered, and she shot him a withering look. "Don't talk."

He smiled and waited until she aimed again. "You know, if you want the teddy bear that badly, I could win it for you."

"I'll win it myself, thanks."

"Oka-a-ay," he said, and watched as she missed.

She swore with impressive skill, then dug into her pocket again. Came up empty. Swore some more.

"My offer still stands." He smiled when she bared her teeth at him. "If you're interested. I'll win it for you."

"Sure you will."

He put a hand to his chest. "Your doubt wounds me. But you should know, I was all-city dart champ."

Cocking a hip, she crossed her arms over her chest. "Really."

"Really."

"So you'll win me the teddy bear."

"Just said so, didn't I?"

She studied him, then let out a little laugh. "Okay, cocky man, what happens then? After you win?"

"I hand you the prize."

"And?"

"And..." He let out a slow, wicked grin, both because he could taste victory and because she was so incredibly hot. And fun. That was the shocker. He was having fun with her. "And in return, *you* give *me* a prize."

Her eyes narrowed to little slits. "Which would be what exactly?"

"I don't know yet. I'll think about it." He slapped down a buck, accepted his three darts. Aimed.

And was stopped by a hand on his arm. He looked into deep green eyes that held a world of knowledge. "I don't want the teddy bear."

"Liar," he said softly, and hit the first balloon. "But that's okay. The bear will look good on my bed." He hit the second balloon.

Pop.

She tossed back her hair. Looked at him with fire-spitting eyes. Then caved. "Okay, damn you, I want the bear.'' Her fingers dug into his arm. ''Name your price.''

They weren't touching—other than her fingernails digging into his biceps, that is—but their mouths were only a fraction apart. Hers was all glossy and smelled like peaches.

He loved peaches.

Their breath comingled, and with a sharp stab of lust he remembered exactly how good those lips tasted. He wanted another taste. ''My price?'' He lifted the third remaining dart. Weighed it in his hand. ''A kiss.''

A laugh escaped her. ''Just a kiss? You don't aim very high for yourself, do you?''

''On the contrary…'' He narrowed his gaze, studied the distance to the remaining balloon. Hefted the dart. ''I know exactly what I want. And I'm not afraid to get it.'' Turning his head, he shot her a last look. ''How about you?''

''I know what I want.''

''The teddy bear.'' He smiled. ''But I've discovered I want it, too.'' He aimed, but before he could throw the dart she stopped him.

''Fine,'' she said.

He set down the dart. ''Fine what?''

''You want me to say it?''

''Yep.''

That earned him a roll of her eyes. ''If you win the bear, I'll give you a kiss for it. Okay? Right here, right now.''

"Oh, no," he said with a shake of his head. "Not right here."

"Where then?"

"Where I say."

She looked him over. Wanted to tell him to go to hell, he could tell. "You have twenty-four hours to claim it, big boy, or all bets are off."

"Deal." He leaned close and she tilted her head back, away from him. Lifting a finger, she wagged it in his face. "Gotta win it first, ace."

He arched a brow, then showed her he was just leaning in to grab the dart.

She crossed her arms and didn't offer another word.

He smiled and tossed the dart.

And won the girl the bear.

Handing it to her, he grinned and said, "You're welcome." He watched as she turned away and buried her face into the bear's neck, her arms hugging the thing tight. Because suddenly his throat was tight as well, he cleared it. "So... Are we going steady now?"

"In your dreams." She huffed off, a vision in her little sundress, her blond hair flying everywhere, arms wrapped around the huge bear.

The kid running the booth watched her go. "That was amazing, dude."

"Yeah." But all Tag could think about was his prize. And it was walking away.

So he did what any red-blooded, aroused man would do. He followed her.

CASSIE STALKED through the carnival, glaring at any man who so much as looked at her. And there were plenty. Women looked, too, if her itchy shoulder blades were any indication. Good. Let them look at bad-ass, no-good, trouble-seeking Cassie Tremaine.

The high-heeled sandals had been a mistake, she thought now, because she couldn't really motor in the them. *Should have worn tennis shoes.*

Had she even packed tennis shoes?

"Cassie."

Oh, that voice.

"Cassie, wait up."

Nope. She kept walking, smiling as though she was the queen of the ball, as if the sexiest, most obnoxious man she'd ever met wasn't striding behind her.

He'd won her the teddy bear. Not only that, her heart had gone all pitter-pattery watching him do it. Unacceptable, really. She had no need for a man doing something she was capable of doing for herself. She wasn't like her mother, damn it.

She had no need for a man, period. Never had. Not knowing who her father was, having never had a positive male role model, having never had men do anything but drool when they looked at her, she supposed she had a rather low view of men in general, but not one had ever proven her wrong. Not yet anyway.

At least Tag wasn't wearing his uniform. Maybe that was the trouble, she thought now. Because without the uniform she obviously couldn't be trusted to remember she didn't like him.

The carnival wasn't that big, and before she knew it she was in the parking lot. Good thing she'd gone and dunked Stacie before going for the teddy bear, because she was good and ready to leave now.

But not to go home. Home was dark and lonely, with only a grumpy cat waiting for her. And nightmares of Pete finding her.

The night was still and hot. She'd give just about anything for a cool breeze. And that's when she decided.

The lake.

It wasn't a very far walk, and her feet were tougher than they looked. She wanted to see the lake by moonlight, and what she wanted, she got. She started off, hugging the teddy bear, not listening in the least for Tag's footsteps. But even if she had been, they weren't there to hear.

Good. He'd gone away. Just as she wanted.

Bastard.

The moment she stepped off the road and onto the little sandy beach, she set down the teddy bear—careful that it didn't get covered in sand—and kicked off her sandals. Her toes dug into the wet sand and she nearly moaned at the cool pleasure of it. *This*. This is what she'd needed. She walked to the water, letting it lap at her ankles.

Alone. "His loss," she told the moon.

"Not yet, it's not."

She was not going to scream, jump, or give any sign that he'd nearly scared her right out of her skin.

Again. Calmly, with a little smile on her lips, she turned. ''What are you doing?''

''Collecting my prize.'' He stepped close, so very close that she could see the moonlight dancing in his eyes. Could feel the heat of his big, tough body.

Tensing, Cassie waited, because she wouldn't welsh on her promise. She'd pay the price. She held very still, waiting to be grabbed. Groped. Conquered.

But he did none of the above, just stepped even closer, careful not to smash her toes.

''What—''

''Shh,'' he said before sliding his arms around her and putting his mouth to hers. She should have known from their earlier encounter he was different. There was no grabbing, no groping, no conquering. Nothing even close. Yes, his arms were strong and firm, but also loose enough she could wriggle free if she wanted to.

She thought about it for all of one second. He was tall, powerfully built, and smelled like heaven. It wasn't often she stood in a man's embrace with every thought draining out of her head, but it happened now as his hands cupped her face, almost reverently, tipping her head for better access.

Oh, yes, better access was good. So good she arched against him. The sound he made low in his throat caused a mirroring one in hers.

At that, the kiss went instantly explosive. His tongue slid home. He hauled her body up against his. And still, she didn't want to be free. The opposite, she realized dimly, snaking her arms around his neck to hold on tight.

With the touch of her fingers on the back of his neck, he groaned, a very erotic sound, and nibbled at her lower lip.

Ohmigod, was all Cassie could think, and then she couldn't have repeated even that. Her knees wobbled; her heart rammed against her ribs as they practically ate each other alive. This…this—whatever it was they were doing to each other—was far more than she had bargained for, and still it wasn't enough. She wanted more. She, a woman who never wanted more from a man. Never.

It took her a moment to realize he'd released her, and that she stood there weaving like a drunk.

"Thank you," he said very politely, in direct contrast to the way he was breathing as if he'd run five miles. Uphill. "That was…"

"Yeah." She licked her lips, tasting him on her. "That was…" Craving his mouth back on hers, she licked her lips again.

He made another rough sound, almost a growl. "Unless you want to extend that price you negotiated, don't."

"Don't…?"

"Don't look at me as if I'm the first one who's ever kissed you stupid. Don't stand there weaving weakly with lust… Ah, hell. Don't even breathe. Yeah, that should do it." He turned from her, shoved his hands through his hair and stared out at the lake.

Shocked, she looked at him. Really looked at him—at his stiff shoulders, his rough breathing—and knew he was as out of control as she was.

And how annoying was it that she no longer wanted him just so that she could cross another item off her revenge list. She wanted him because...well, just because. "It got a little out of hand, that's all."

He shot her a look of disgust over his shoulder. "You think?"

"Yeah."

Before she knew what he was about, he turned, lifted a hand and caressed her cheek. "So it wouldn't, couldn't, happen again, right?"

She barely caught herself from closing her eyes and sighing at the surprising tenderness of his big, warm hand. "Of course not."

"Liar," he whispered softly. Before she could snarl at him for that, he walked away.

5

TWO DAYS LATER Tag still couldn't get that kiss out of his head. It went with him to work, to play, to bed...and that's where it was the worst. Bed.

He wanted Cassie there with him, he couldn't deny that. He wanted her badly.

But why? She was bad attitude personified. She hated everything about him, his life, his job.

So what did that say about him, being so undeniably attracted to her?

That he was sick, very sick.

But knowing it didn't stop the desire, so that when he walked into his office after a day from hell, desperately in need of coffee and some time off, and saw her standing there in front of his receptionist, his gut took a hungry leap.

He told himself it was simply because she exuded sex appeal and it had been...well, longer than it should have since his last sexual experience.

It was the outfit, he decided. She wore a microskirt the color of a field of daffodils, and a matching zippered crop-top, out of which came two spaghetti straps from what he assumed was a bathing suit worn beneath. Her hair had been piled on top of her head, with strands tumbling free to her shoulders. And then there were her legs—long and toned and bare except for a pair of strappy sandals.

"I was just wondering if the restraining order I took out in New York protects me here," she was saying, and all Tag's lusty thoughts flew right out the window. "Because I've received some more threatening mail and—"

"What restraining order?" Tag asked, moving close. "What threatening mail?" She smelled like coconut oil. He loved coconut oil. Ordering himself not to notice her scent, or to picture what she was obviously dressed for—sunbathing—he looked into her green, green eyes.

"If you don't mind, I'm having a conversation with your receptionist," she said. "A *private* conversation."

Roxy, who'd been working at the station since his father had been sheriff, shot him a sympathetic look, then turned back to Cassie. "You do have a restraining order already in place? In New York, you said, right? Can you give us the details?"

Cassie glance sideways at Tag. "Us?"

"Well, the sheriff here is really good at what he does," Roxy assured her. "He can help protect you— we just need to know what's going on. We'll need to know who the restraining order is for, what specifically, and any other pertinent details for our records."

"Such as why you didn't tell me when you first hit town," Tag said lightly, not feeling light at all.

Cassie picked up the purse she'd set on the counter. "You know what? Never mind."

"But—" Roxy made a frustrated sound when Cassie pivoted away and headed toward the door.

"Thanks anyway," Cassie called over her shoulder.

Not even her curvy little ass could sidetrack him now. With one last glance at Roxy, who lifted her shoulders to indicate she knew as much as he did, he followed Cassie.

Who gave no indication that she even noticed.

"Cassie," he said as she strode out of the station and into the early evening.

Her heels clicked on the asphalt. Everyone she passed took a good long second look, both men and women. Some started talking. Cassie didn't so much as look at a single one of them.

"Cassie," he said again, but as she was having no part of him, it left him following her like some damn puppy dog. But she'd tweaked his curiosity—and concern—and if there was anything more dogged than a curious, concerned cop, he didn't know what it was.

At her car, she opened her purse. Slid on sunglasses.

"Cassie."

Pulling out her keys, she opened her door, and would have slid inside if he hadn't put a hand on her waist.

Going still, she stared down at his hand, which looked large and imposing on the paler, softer skin of her very tantalizing middle. "I paid the debt the other night," she said very quietly. "We're even, remember?"

With a rather unprofessional oath, he dropped his hand. "Do you think I care about that?"

"You've got a penis, don't you?"

He sucked in a slow careful breath because something about her stoked his temper every time. "You wanted the teddy bear, I won it for you."

"Thank you Mr. He-Man. And I paid your price."

"That's right," he said, keeping his voice even with effort. "End of story."

"Then why are we still talking about it?"

"Because you brought it up!" Lord, she could try the patience of a saint. He took a deep breath. "I want to hear about the restraining order. About your threatening mail."

"Yeah, well that was a private conversation and you were eavesdropping." But she seemed less hostile now and he forced himself to relax.

Forced himself to be the calm cop he knew he was. And once he did that, he had to admit it bugged the hell out of him that she thought he'd insist on more "payment" for that damn teddy bear.

Had she really never met a guy who didn't want something from her? He knew she didn't have a father around—never had. He knew what Biff had wanted from her. But what about others? Hadn't there been others? Anyone who'd just been there for her? Given her attitude, he had to doubt it. That thought unsettled him to the core, and if the kiss hadn't so rocked his world, he might have spared a moment to feel guilty he'd asked her for that much.

Then he realized something else, that she was avoiding looking at him, and when he took a good look, he saw why.

She was uncomfortable around him. Interesting. If she'd paid the debt, and it was as over as she'd said, why wouldn't she look at him? "Cassie, talk to me." He paused. "Please."

With an exaggerated sigh, she tipped her head and looked skyward. "You know me. Wild Cassie Tremaine. I go looking for trouble. Just ask anyone."

"Pleasantville isn't Mayberry," Tag said. "We have our fair share of village idiots." With his cousin leading the pack.

"Surely you've heard the stories."

"And I sincerely doubt any of them are true."

Her gaze jerked up to his. Oh, yeah, he'd managed to surprise her. Had no one ever believed in her?

"I'm just having some trouble with an obsessed guy, that's all," she said finally.

"A fan?"

"Sort of."

This he didn't like. He imagined, given her chosen occupation, she faced similar problems all the time. That she actually needed a restraining order was deeply disturbing. "How serious is the trouble?"

She lifted a shoulder and didn't look at him.

"Serious enough for a restraining order." He turned her to face him, left his hands on her bare upper arms because he wanted her unsettled enough to talk. "I can find out with or without you, but I'd rather you tell me."

"It's not that big of a deal." She shrugged him off. "I'm safe here. Nothing bad can happen in Pleasantville, right…*Sheriff?*"

"Do you have a thing against all cops or just me?"

"Oh, definitely all cops, but especially second generation ones."

It wasn't the first time he'd wondered. "You know my father."

"I grew up here, didn't I? Right here in good old Pleasantville, where, like I said, nothing bad could ever happen." Her laugh didn't convince him, but mostly because it wasn't humor in her eyes now but…hurt? If he had to guess, he'd have said plenty of bad things had happened to her, right here in Pleasantville.

"Look, I just…had a long night last night and got a little spooked. Okay?"

"I can't imagine you being spooked for anything less than a good reason."

"I know. I'm so tough I'd scare away the mob."

She didn't look so tough right now. "Cassie. You're scaring me."

"Look, Pete's just a typical guy. He thought he

could have something I didn't want to give him, and he's pissed. He'll get over it.''

"Pete. A...lover?"

She ripped off her sunglasses, her eyes gleaming. ''None of your damn business. Now if you'll excuse me, I'm headed to the lake for some time alone.''

"It's going to be getting dark soon."

"Thanks, Einstein."

He looked into the open convertible. Miss Priss lay asleep on the passenger seat, next to a picnic basket and a book. *"The Rogue's Kiss?"* he asked in surprise, staring at the historical romance novel with the half-naked guy on the cover.

"Do you think underwear models can't read?"

"You read...romance?"

"Shockers, isn't it?"

What was shocking was the layers to her. Who'd have thought Cassie Tremaine would have a romantic side?

She sank into the car, started it. "Unless you didn't meet your ticket quota for the week, back off. I'd hate to run over those toes on my way outta here."

Risking it, he held open her door. "Is that why you're in town? To get out of the limelight for a while to avoid this guy?"

"I'm in town opening—"

"Bare Essentials. Yeah, yeah." He gripped the hand that would have slid on her sunglasses again. "I'm not buying that anymore, Cassie. You're here because you're scared. How long are you staying?"

"Until I feel like hitting the road again. Now move."

He did, only because he felt the tremble in her fingers and it shocked him. Vulnerability? He'd seen a flash of it before and dismissed it because it was unthinkable. The smart-ass, tough-as-hell Cassie couldn't be vulnerable.

Or was she? He couldn't help but feel that he'd missed something about her. That there was more to the tall, incredibly beautiful, distant woman than she wanted everyone to see.

He watched her peel out of the parking lot, heading toward the lake. It frustrated him that he'd been unable to figure out who the hell she really was.

He went back inside the station, thinking maybe he'd just try harder.

Roxy looked at him with a raised brow. "What's up with the lingerie lady?"

"I haven't a clue."

"You'd better get one."

"Why do you say that?"

"Well..." Roxy glanced at the door, a worried look on her face. "I know people like to whisper about her behind her back, talk about her like she was the wild child from hell all those years ago..."

"And?"

"And I think it was just that...talk. I think she's got guts, coming back here. She holds her head up like it doesn't matter what people say, but..."

He sighed, because Roxy was always like this, always had to be coaxed out of her stories. "But?"

"But she's scared, Sheriff. A woman like that, who's been through so much…she doesn't get scared easily. And yet she is."

Tag thought about that as he changed out of his uniform. As he promised himself pizza and a beer. But then the funniest thing happened.

His car drove to the lake, just as the sun took its final dip beneath the horizon. Bypassing the popular swimming hole, he drove around to the east side, where a quiet bay surrounded by trees and growth made a more private area.

It was where he'd kissed Cassie only a few nights before.

He parked next to the only other car around, a sunshine-yellow Porsche.

It was open and unlocked, and he shook his head. She should be more careful. He stopped to stroke Miss Priss, who stretched, purred, and went right back to sleep on the passenger seat. "If only your mistress was as easy to please," he said, then headed off on the trail down to the beach.

The night was a dark one already, with just a few silvery clouds. The heat from the day hadn't begun to fade, which was why the sound of the water hitting the shore in gentle waves made him yearn to dive in.

The small bay was deserted—unless he counted the sexy mermaid playing around in the water. She popped up about twenty feet out, her back to him.

Her long wet hair clung to her shoulders, which gleamed in the meager light. Tipping her head back to the night sky, her eyes were closed, and on her face was an expression he'd never seen before.

Contentment.

Then she bent to dive deep. For a second he had the magnificent view of her backside, and the small patch of wet material dividing the most perfect set of buns he'd ever seen.

Then she was gone.

He stared at the water, waiting for her to surface, and she didn't disappoint. She came up only about five feet out now, and facing him. "I already ate the picnic," she said, treading water.

"I'm not hungry." For food, that is.

Still treading water, she studied him, only her elegant neck and face showing. "You coming in?"

And have that long, sleek, wet body within reach? Slowly he shook his head. "That would be a bad idea."

"No bathing suit, huh?"

"No."

"That can be fixed." She reached behind her back for a moment, then flung something that landed at his feet.

He scooped up two tiny triangles and some string, dangled it from his fingers. Her bikini top.

His mouth went dry.

Then something equally wet hit him in the chest. Catching it with his other hand, he held up...her bottoms. This time it wasn't just his mouth that reacted. "What are you doing?"

"Treading water. Naked." She smiled the smile of an angel.

And if he could have, he would have laughed. *"Cassie."*

"You sure say my name a lot. Don't worry, slick. Your virtue is safe with me. I just thought I'd put us on even playing ground. You can strip down and come in now."

Hallelujah, cried his body.

Holy shit, cried his mind.

Good thing his mind was in control, barely. "You want me to come in. Without my clothes."

"Unless you want to get them wet."

"I want to talk about your visit to the station. What the hell is going on?"

Instead of answering, she floated on her back for a moment before executing a perfect back somersault. At the flash of generous breasts, then flat belly, then...he nearly swallowed his tongue. Tan lines. She had lots of tan lines.

He loved tan lines. Christ, just shoot him now.

"Are you coming?" she asked when she surfaced.

Nearly in his pants. "About the restraining order—"

"I'm tired of shouting."

"So you'll talk to me if I come in."

"You're quick, Tag."

"Uh-huh." He didn't believe her. "Why are you being…nice?"

She blinked at that.

"Is it because I'm not in my uniform?"

Now those eyes chilled and she dipped down to her chin. "Your uniform has nothing to do with this."

"Really?" Ripping his T-shirt over his head, his hands went to the buttons on his Levi's. To hell with being stoic. To hell with restraint. To hell with not taking what he wanted when it was being offered to him. "Then why do you only talk to me when I'm out of it?"

"Because I don't like it?"

He undid his first button, watching her watch him very closely, the desire unmistakable. Good. She wanted him, too. They could scratch this itch and get it the hell out of their way. But he wanted to hear her say it, wanted to hear that she wanted him as much as he wanted her.

"You look hot." She splashed him, just a little.

And he opened another button. "You want to watch what you start, Cassie."

"Oh, I'm watching." And she was. She hit him with another splash.

Another button.

More desire.

"Get in the water, Tag. Cool off." With that, she allowed the very tips of her breasts to break the surface.

His eyes narrowed into dangerous slits as he kicked off his shoes and socks.

Then shoved off the rest of his clothes.

And my, oh, my, Cassie thought, her body humming already, he looked amazing naked. She splashed him again for the sheer pleasure of watching water running down his big, strong, sleek form in little rivulets she suddenly wanted to lick off. Broad, tanned shoulders, hard chest tapering to a narrow waist, powerful legs…and what lay between those thighs made her breath catch. "Coming?"

"Oh, yeah."

Oh, yeah. With any luck, they'd both come.

She needed this, she decided. She deserved it. And afterward, she'd feel better. More relaxed. They could go back to ignoring each other. But damn, he looked good strutting into the deliciously cool water without so much as a wince, never breaking eye contact, until, a few feet from her, he vanished into the water.

With the lack of a moon, she couldn't see where he was headed, but she wasn't stupid. Braced and ready, she let out only a cool smile when he surfaced again, slowly, confidently, only a fraction of an inch in front of her.

He shook his hair back. Water ran down his jaw. A jaw she suddenly wanted to touch. Strange, that urge. Sex was a tool and only a tool. A stimulus. A muscle relaxant. A great way to guarantee a good night's sleep.

Nothing more.

So this urge to be tender bugged the hell out of her. Forget tender. She wanted hard and fast, and then she wanted him gone. To facilitate the matter, she put her arms over his shoulders, letting him do all the work to keep them afloat.

It also slid their bodies in direct contact. Chest to chest, thigh to thigh, and everything in between. And oh, baby, was there a lot in between. Her nipples brushed the light hair on his chest. His legs entangled with hers. And his erection... Mmm, she slid it between her legs, loving the feeling of having him there. He was hot, pulsing. Huge. And it wasn't easy to keep her eyes open on his, to keep her thoughts straight, when her entire body had melted so that she had no bones left.

"Cassie." One large hand danced down her spine, cupped her bottom and pressed her against his hot, hard body as he supported her weight. "I'm ready to hear about the restraining order," he said very quietly, keeping them above water with no apparent effort.

"I..." He had his hand on her ass, his penis between her legs. "Um..." Her heart was pounding dully in her ears. Her nipples had long ago pebbled to hard, needy beads. And between her clenched thighs she was creamy. Rational thought escaped her and he hadn't done anything yet. "What?"

He let out a slow, knowing smile.

Damn him and his unbearable control. Well, she had enough left to know she had to destroy it. Sinking her fingers into his hair, she shifted even closer so their mouths were just touching. "So. You really want to…" She wrapped her legs around his waist, thrilling to his quickly indrawn breath. "Talk?"

Now both hands held her bottom, hard, his fingers squeezing. She was so close to him they'd melted together. And because she'd spread her legs wide, wrapping them around his waist so satisfactorily, the tip of his penis…oh, yes, nearly slid home.

Nearly. Because he held back. Everything. "You want me?" he asked, his voice rough and serrated, his mouth so close to hers, but not close enough. His hands still gripped her bottom, holding her slightly away, so that his wonderfully hot, hard, huge erection only teased the very center of her universe.

"I think that's fairly obvious," she answered.

"Then talk to me."

"Uh…"

Looking fierce and hot, and so damn sexy she wanted to gobble him up in one bite, he stroked her again. This time his chest lightly brushed her nipples, and she could barely breathe.

"Maybe you skipped the birds and the bees lesson," she said. "But you should know, talking has little to do with wanting you."

He looked down at her breasts, two hard, aching points brushing against his chest, and groaned. Slowly he lifted her up a little, dipping his head so he could rub his jaw across the very tips. "Can Pete find you here?"

No, she wouldn't talk about this, even if he'd forced a pathetic, needy whimper from her throat.

"Cassie?" Another little stroke with his not-so-little penis. Her entire body quivered, dancing on the very edge of an orgasm she wanted with all her heart.

"Can he?" he growled.

She stared down at his mouth, wanting it on hers. At the look, he groaned low and deep. His fingers, still supporting her, glided farther down her backside and dipped between her legs. Unerringly found her flash point.

Unable to help herself, she thrust against him and he groaned again, the sound melding with hers. She'd never had an orgasm without purposeful, calculated thought before, and yet here she was, quivering on the very edge without a thought in her head other than...*more, please, more.*

They weren't very far out in the water. Not too far to miss the fact that her cell phone was ringing. She stared at the spot where she'd left it while he stared at her.

"You get a lot of calls?" he asked hoarsely.

"Very few now that I'm off work." She closed her eyes, then jerked them open when she felt his mouth slide over hers in a far too brief kiss.

Bending his head, he sighed and rubbed his jaw lightly over her breasts, making them both moan again. "Get it," he said and with one last perfectly aimed stroke with his fingers, gently unwrapped her legs from around him. "It might be important."

Walking out of the water, feeling him alongside her, Cassie wondered at the amazing control of the man. She wondered how he'd gotten that way, and—

And all else fell from her mind as she scooped up the phone from her towel. She'd missed the call. But the caller had a New York area code that didn't belong to her agent. And then the phone rang again... same number. "Hello?" she said.

"Hello, Cassie," said Pete. "I'm here and you're not."

Cassie looked up into Tag's face and felt the blood drain from her own.

6

_____

"YOU HAVEN'T CALLED," Pete said in a congenial voice. "Even though I know you had some...car trouble before you left. Why didn't you call, Cassie?"

Very aware that Tag stood less than a foot away, still as gloriously naked as was she, Cassie didn't say a word. Pete's voice gave her goose bumps, as did his casual reference to how he'd slashed her tires.

"We're friends," he went on. "_Friends,_ Cassie. And we're so much more than that, too. Did you know I haven't come to find you, not because I couldn't, but because I wanted you to come find me?"

His words disturbed her, made her feel sick. She'd liked this man, had let him into her life, and that her instincts had been so far off, so wrong, cut deeply.

"We belong together, you know this," Pete said in her ear. "We were meant to be. I'm going to make it happen."

Her skin crawled. "No—"

"Yes." His voice hardened. "You can't treat me this way, Cassie, vanishing from my world like this. It's not okay. Friends don't do that to one another."

"Friends." Suddenly she felt cold, so very cold, and she grabbed for something to cover herself. That it happened to be Tag's T-shirt didn't stop her; she shoved it over her wet head and body, then wrapped her free arm around herself. "Funny you use that word. I don't have any."

"Cassie." His voice was low now, conciliatory, quick to soothe. "Just tell me where you are, I can make it all up to you."

He was insane. And she hadn't seen it until it had been almost too late. "Don't call me again, Pete." She clicked off, tossed the phone down by her sandals, and stared off into the night, telling herself he still had no idea where she was or he'd have come for her by now.

Tag came up beside her. He was still looking at her with his sharp, probing gaze, still naked and apparently unconcerned about that fact. She knew male models, tons of them, and had never seen a man so comfortable in his own skin. He was beautiful, and the way he looked at her...in another place and time she might have been tempted to let herself weaken for him.

Who was she fooling? She *had* weakened for him, had very nearly trusted him with anything he wanted to do. Good God, what was wrong with her? He was a sheriff, of all things, a man with authority and power over her if he so chose, and more than that, he was his father's son. No doubt Sheriff Sean Taggart couldn't be trusted any more than Richard could be, and yet she'd nearly...

He pulled his jeans over his still-wet body but didn't fasten them. He looked like a Greek god standing there next to her, staring out into the night.

Until he turned to look at her. Those eyes of his weren't a god's. They were a cop's. "Pete."

"Yes."

"Another threat?"

"He's upset because he can't find me."

"Well, thank God for small favors." When she didn't answer, he sighed, put his hands on her and pulled her close. That her body wanted to be even closer felt like a betrayal. "You're not going to ask me for help," he guessed.

"No."

"Then I'm going to ask you." He shook her lightly until she locked gazes with him. "Let me help you, Cassie. *Please*. Let me do this for you."

"I don't need—"

"No, you don't *want*." His hands slid up her arms, cupped her face. "You're independent, I get that. You're proud. I get that, too. But you're not stupid. You need help. We're friends, if nothing else, and—"

"Oh, no." She let out a short mirthless laugh and backed up. "Not you, too."

He narrowed his eyes. "What, is the word *friend* a trigger word for you?"

"I'll admit, we're...almost lovers. Sparring partners, maybe. But not friends." When he stepped close again, she took a shaky breath because her heart suddenly and inexplicably hurt. ''We're not. We'll never be that.''

She saw surprise flash across his features and, damn it, hurt, too, but that wouldn't stop her. It was a dog-eat-dog world and she had to stay on top. ''A man can't be a woman's friend, not—''

''That's bullshit.''

''—when—'' she continued coolly while shaking like a leaf inside. ''Not when all he wants is sex.''

He stopped cold, stared at her. She could see the shock in his eyes. Then he pulled away, turned his back.

Oh, yeah, she'd hit the mark that time. He felt guilty as hell, and that should have been tremendously satisfying. But the victory felt hollow.

''I'm sorry,'' he said.

''It's nothing personal.''

''Like hell.'' But he merely slid his hands into his pockets. ''You came back here to Pleasantville to hide. That's fact. You came here even with bitter childhood memories because you knew one thing… you knew you'd be safe.''

''You don't know a single truth about my past.''

''I would if you told me.''

She wasn't going to tell him anything.

''Fine,'' he said angrily. ''I'll have to guess then, and you have no one to blame but yourself if I'm wrong.''

''You've already heard what I was like.''

"I have." He looked over his shoulder at her, his eyes dark and intense. "But as I've already told you, I think the truth is radically different."

He didn't believe the gossip. So what *did* he believe?

"You were right to come here." He still looked toward the lake. "You'll be safe. You'll come to the station and let someone know if you feel Pete has managed to track you."

"Yes," she told his sleek, still-wet back. The back she'd wanted to touch, wanted to put her mouth to.

She'd tell him anything if he'd go away and leave her be, with her burning eyes and burning throat. "I'll come to the station if I need help."

With one short nod, he bent, scooped up her towel and tossed it to her. He looked at her for a long, long moment, then his lips curved slowly. Solemnly. "Be careful, Cassie."

And then she was alone. Just as she'd wanted.

WELL, HELL, Tag thought, stretching out in the hammock in his vast front yard, studying the stars. He'd certainly learned a few things about himself at the lake tonight, hadn't he. And none of it was anything to be particularly proud of.

First, he'd apparently proven to Cassie that all men were scum. Every one of them. Not that she hadn't apparently already formed that opinion, but he'd definitely enforced it.

What had come over him? Lust, he admitted. A red haze of lust.

She was being stalked for crissake, and what had he done? He'd stripped down to his birthday suit like a hopeful high school kid and dove into that water without a single thought.

Oh, yeah, he deserved her disdain, every ounce of it. But she hadn't deserved his momentary lapse in judgment.

Well, he could fix that much at least. On his way back from the lake he'd gone to the station and done what he could for her, not that she'd appreciate it. He'd arranged for drive-bys at her house. He'd alerted his deputies to the possibility of trouble. And he'd put in a request for a copy of the original report and the restraining order.

She wouldn't thank him, he knew that, but at least he had his head on straight now and wouldn't be distracted from what he had to do.

He wouldn't. No matter how glorious she looked nude, swimming like a mermaid beneath the stars, her satiny skin glistening like a feast as she frolicked unselfconsciously. Her body—a mind-blowing study in curves and feminine delights—was perfection, and he'd seen every bit of it tonight. Rock-hard mauve nipples made for sucking. Rounded hips begging for his hands to grip tight. Long, tanned legs, and the treasure in between that had made his mouth water with hunger.

Just the thought could bring him to his knees, so he stopped thinking.

But he didn't stop dreaming, not that night, and not the next.

He did, however, a few days later, take his weekly phone call from his father, something he would have gladly skipped if he'd only put in Caller ID as he kept meaning to.

"You feeling better?" Tag asked him, knowing his father had been suffering from rheumatory arthritis, and knowing the man would never admit it.

"I'll live, unfortunately. You keeping the streets clean of stupidity, son?"

Tag let out a silent sigh and rubbed his temples. "What do you think?"

"I think I shouldn't have retired. Heard Cassie Tremaine Montgomery is back in town. The slut."

Tag went utterly still. "She left here right after high school. What was she, maybe seventeen? Don't you think you're being a little harsh?"

"What do you know about it? You were at college when she left. Trust me. Keep your eye on her."

That didn't seem to be a problem. What *was* a problem was the fact that he wanted to keep more than his eyes on her. He wanted his hands, his mouth and his body on her, as well.

"What's happening at work?" his father asked.

"The usual," Tag said. "Just a D.U.I. at the moment."

"Any ongoing cases?"

"Nothing I can't handle."

"Sure?"

Tag counted to ten. "Positive."

"Okay, then. I've got to go."

"Sure. But in case you were wondering, I'm fine."

"I know you're fine. If you weren't I'd hear about it. It's work I want to know about. You'd best be doing a good job, upholding our family name."

Or what? Tag wondered wearily. He'd swing his authority around like a belt? He rubbed his temples. "I'll talk to you next week."

"You haven't been out to see me."

Tag hadn't, that was true. He hadn't been able to take the hour or so of verbal abuse he'd no doubt have to sit through before being dismissed like a worthless underling.

He bit his tongue on the harsh words he wanted to say. He wouldn't act like his father. "I've got to go, Dad." Hanging up the phone, he gave in to a brief moment of self-hatred for not telling his father to just go to hell.

Pretty pathetic. Thirty-two years old and he still had a deep desire to have a picture-perfect family life with warm, loving people around him.

Or one loving person. The one he hadn't found yet—his fantasy wife. The thought made him huff out a mirthless laugh because he was no closer to finding her than he was to really living in Mayberry, U.S.A.

KATE ARRIVED, and Cassie had to admit she'd never been happier to see anyone in her entire life. Her cousin hadn't changed at all; she was still the voice of calm reason to Cassie's wild heart.

Physically, they were opposites as well, and Cassie had always admired Kate's long, thick dark hair, her perfect heart face, her sweet smile. Although she hated people thinking so, Kate was sweet everything, and being around her calmed Cassie's restless soul in a way few others could.

On Kate's first night back in Pleasantville they stayed up late, sitting on the floor of the nearly ready Bare Essentials, gorging on pizza and M&M's, going over the plans for their grand opening.

Maybe it was the bottle of wine they shared, or maybe it was simply the sheer delight of seeing each other after too long an absence, but they laughed and talked and listened to music until well past midnight.

Cassie had to give her cousin credit. Kate let Cassie keep the conversation safe. Meaning they talked about Kate. Bare Essentials. And gossiped happily about the people in Pleasantville.

Then the clock struck one and Kate's smile faded as she studied Cassie. "You know I love you, right?"

Ah, hell. "Yep." In case Kate wanted to talk serious, she cranked up the radio to ear-splitting level.

Kate simply lifted that superior brow Cassie was certain had intimidated hundreds of others. "You could tell me anything," she yelled over the music. "You know that."

"I'm fine."

"Yeah." Kate put her hand around her mouth and shouted, "So fine you have purple bruises beneath your eyes." She flicked the radio off. "Delicate ones, of course, because you're the only woman I know who could skip makeup and eat junk food for a week and still look amazing. But I know you, Cassie." She softened her voice and reached for her hand. "Whether you like it or not, I know you're not okay."

"Kate—"

"You haven't asked for your mail." She reached into her purse and came up with a handful of letters. All addressed to her. All from Pete. "You should be giving these to the local authorities."

"The authorities here know about him." Deciding she was done with this conversation, Cassie stood and stretched, and caught sight of a car pulling up out front.

Not just any car, but a police squad car. Damn it.

She tucked Pete's letters into her purse and turned with her hands on her hips as one tall, dark and sinfully fine-looking Sheriff Sean Taggart entered the building with a casual nonchalance that made her every hormone stand up and quiver.

Take what you can, honey, and spit the rest back out. Cassie thought about what Flo would say and had to admit there wasn't much to spit back out when it came to Tag.

Not exactly a comfort.

"Fancy you showing up out here," she drawled

slowly though her heart had started racing at just the sight of him. She hadn't seen him since that night at the lake when he'd stripped down and showed her he was one pretty remarkable male specimen. When she'd accused him of only wanting sex. When she'd nearly succumbed to temptation and let herself lean on someone. *Him.*

Kate's head was swiveling as she looked back and forth between the two of them. "I take it you two know each other."

Tag just stared at Cassie, and she sighed. "Kate, meet Sheriff Sean Taggart. The man who single-handedly tripled my car insurance rates."

"Well, then." Kate smiled and held out her hand. "Nice to meet the rare person who can get the best of my cousin." When Tag nodded, then looked back at Cassie, unmistakable trouble in his gaze, Kate grabbed her purse. "Oka-a-ay. I'm thinking now is a good time to get some shut-eye."

"Kate—"

"I have a feeling you're in good hands," she whispered, then hugged Cassie tight before she vanished.

"You scared her off," Cassie accused.

"If she's related to you, she's no more scared of me than she would be of a kitten," Tag said evenly.

"Why are you here?"

"Because of the five complaints logged about the volume of your music."

"I turned it down." She turned her back. "I'll behave now. You can go."

"I'll just wait while you lock up."

"Oh, I'm not leaving yet." She bent to stroke Miss Priss. "I have some stock to go through, and—" She squeaked in surprise when he whipped her around to face him.

"Damn it to hell," he muttered, staring down into her face.

"Damn what to hell?" she asked, pure frost in her voice.

Her shoulders were stiff in Tag's hands, but it had just come to him. The problem he'd been stumbling over since she'd strode into town.

Yeah, he wanted her, just as she'd accused. But he also...*liked* her. More than that, he wanted her to trust him.

She didn't, not even close, but she would. He was suddenly quite determined about that.

"You know what I think?" he asked her softly. "I think your kick-ass demeanor, as well as the job that's made you so famous, is all a front."

She stared at him as if he was crazy. "What?"

"Beneath all that wild sensuality and come-hither smile designed to make grown men beg, you're all talk."

"Excuse me?"

"You just stroked the cat. I saw you."

"So?"

"So you claim to hate that cat. You claim to hate this town, and yet here you still are. Oh, yeah, I'm on to something all right. You're not nearly as untamed and uncaring as you want people to believe, not even close." Sure of himself, he smiled. "In fact, you're just one great big fraud."

She let out a disbelieving laugh. "You have no idea what you're talking about. I'm as out there as they come, just ask anyone."

"Not buying it. You're all talk, Cassie Tremaine Montgomery. All talk."

"You think so?" She grabbed a box off a shelf, tossed it to the floor, then kneeled down to riffle through it. "I'll show you talk." She lifted a set of handcuffs. "I have a set of these in my bedroom. Waiting for the right evening, the right lover."

He nearly swallowed his tongue, and instead lifted a shoulder. "So what? I have a pair on me all day long."

A sound of frustration passed her kissable lips as she tossed the handcuffs over her shoulder and pawed through the box again. With a cry of triumph, she help up a small plastic package holding…

He gulped hard.

"A clit ring," she said. "I have one of these, too."

"Are…you wearing it now?"

Her triumph faded, and with a growl she tossed it over her shoulder to fall next to the discarded handcuffs, leaving him to give a silent thanks because he doubted he could have handled remaining so calm, cool and collected if she'd showed him a clit ring.

On her clit.

Just the thought made him break a sweat.

Cassie dove back into the box, and this time came up with a small white leather pack and a smile that went right to his crotch.

Lord help him, he'd opened Pandora's box.

"Know what this is?" she asked in a sultry voice. "A portable vibrator. For the woman on the go. It fits into a pocket or small purse."

Oh, man. He leaned back against the wall, crossed his arms and forced himself to yawn. She would not goad him into a physical relationship, not when she still believed he wanted her only for sex. Nope. He wouldn't touch her.

At his feigned boredom, she sputtered. "You think I wouldn't use this to make myself come?"

He just lifted a brow.

Still on her knees, she shot him a look of pure daring, which in truth started his heart pumping, even before she lifted her denim skirt, revealing a tiny patch of red satin masquerading as panties. Pulling out the small white vibrator, she turned it on, smiled the very smile of the devil, and ran it over her thigh before settling it directly between her legs.

"Mmm," she whispered, letting her head fall back on her shoulders. Her eyes closed as she slowly moved the vibrator up and down and back again.

Her breath came quicker, and so did his. "Cassie—"

"Shh." Her hips started pumping in tune to her hand.

His own hands fisted.

"God. This is so much better than a fumbling man."

He'd show her fumbling.

"Oh, yeah…" The vibrator hummed. Her hand moved faster.

She moaned softly.

Up and down.

The red satin became wet, he could see it.

And Tag nearly sank to the floor. "Cassie—"

Her mouth fell open, her tongue came out and wet her lips. Her breath caught and she went still, so utterly still…then shuddered as she let out a little helpless cry, lost in her own pleasure.

Tag didn't move a muscle, he couldn't.

After a moment she opened sleepy, sated eyes and smiled. "Definitely much better than a man." With a click she turned off the vibrator and let her skirt fall back down.

Before she could riffle through the box again, his brain started functioning, barely, and he came forward. "Uncle," he said hoarsely, hauling her to her feet. "I get it. You're not all talk. And you're killing me. Lock up, you're going home."

"I suppose you think you're going to tuck me in and sing me a lullaby."

"No. You're going home alone."

"Suit yourself."

No mistaking her anger that he hadn't fallen at her feet in a boneless mass of need, but no one had ever wanted her for anything besides sex, and he refused to fit into the same mold as all the other assholes in her life.

"Got your keys?" he asked calmly, as if he couldn't have hammered steel with his raging erection.

She pocketed the vibrator and shot him a long look, definitely noticing the problem behind his zipper. "I have my keys." She patted the vibrator. "In fact, I have everything I need, thank you very much."

Fine. She was pissed at him, nothing new. But it was satisfying, despite the burning need of his body, to see the shock in her eyes that he wasn't going to try to get into her very wet panties.

And he would hold firm. At least for tonight.

7

WITH KATE IN TOWN to help get Bare Essentials going, Cassie felt free to give in to impulse.

And impulse had her eating whatever she wanted—screw her agent telling her to remain thin—which included a daily sandwich by Diane at the deli. Impulse had her going to the library for more of the books she sucked down every night—and teasing Mrs. Wilkens about her phone sex.

And impulse sent her back to New York for her agent's birthday party bash.

Going back had nothing to do with work. Nothing to do with needing something from her apartment. Or even wanting to see her friends.

Neither did it mean that she missed New York, because actually, surprisingly, she hadn't given it that much thought.

She just needed...out.

And she made no mistake about it, she knew exactly why she needed out. Tag.

She still couldn't believe he'd sent her home alone after she'd teased herself into a feverous pitch in front of him. Granted she hadn't shown as much skin as she had at the lake, when she'd worn nothing *but* skin...but she'd masturbated right in front of him! She knew men, damn it, and knew that watching a woman touch herself was basically nirvana. Heaven on earth. A fantasy come true.

She'd given him that, and still, he'd remained cool as rain. Nearly a week had gone by and she still couldn't believe he hadn't given in to his body's obvious craving.

But he hadn't, at least not in front of her.

Which meant he had far more self-control and restraint than she did, and she had plenty. It startled her, knowing he wasn't the usual puppet on a string. That he had his own mind. Was his own man.

It startled her, and unsettled her. Enough that she told Kate she was going for two days. She needed some action, and New York was where it was at.

Kate wasn't happy, but Cassie easily distracted her, mostly because Kate was busy with other projects such as working at the local theater—the Rialto—not to mention she had her own problems with the sexy Jack Winfield. And he *was* pretty damn sexy, so Cassie could understand the distraction.

In any case, Cassie wasn't worried. She wouldn't be in New York long enough for Pete to track her down. Besides, she had the restraining order. And in the mood she found herself in, she felt invincible.

Or at least, battle ready. *Bring it on, Pete,* she thought testily. *Bring it on.*

Back in the city, she looked up her friends, went

to the birthday party, hit a great new dance club afterward, lined up some work for the fall and winter...and by the end of forty-eight hours, was ready to go home.

Home. As in Ohio.

Pleasantville, Ohio. She sat on the plane, staring sightlessly down as the landscape passed her by, wondering when exactly she had started to think of that one-horse, narrow-minded, too small town as her... *home?*

Not good. In the name of distraction, she asked the flight attendant for a deck of cards and tried to occupy herself in a mean game of solitaire, but she kept losing.

By the time she got off the plane, shouldered her carry-on and walked outside, the sun was setting. She put on her sunglasses and looked for Kate, who'd promised to pick her up, and realized she was still carrying the deck of cards.

Maybe she'd get Kate to come over to play a game with her tonight. Then she wouldn't have to stay up late and stare into the mirror above the bed wondering what the hell she was going to do for another long month and a half.

Only there was no sign of Kate. Really, that was no surprise. Cassie had always figured Kate would be late to her own funeral. With a sigh, she found an empty bench and sat, idly shuffling the cards to keep her hands busy.

When a patrol car pulled up, she frowned. Her

Play **LUCKY HEARTS** for this..

exciting FREE gift!
This surprise mystery gift could be yours free

when you play **LUCKY HEARTS!**

...then continue your lucky streak with a sweetheart of a deal!

1. Play Lucky Hearts as instructed on the opposite page.
2. Send back this card and you'll receive 2 brand-new Harlequin Blaze™ books. These books have a cover price of $4.50 each in the U.S., and $5.25 each in Canada, but they are yours to keep absolutely free.
3. There's no catch! You're under no obligation to buy anything. We charge nothing— ZERO—for your first shipment. And you don't have to make any minimum number of purchases—not even one!
4. The fact is thousands of readers enjoy their receiving books by mail from the Harlequin Reader Service®. They enjoy the convenience of home delivery...they like getting the best new novels at discount prices, BEFORE they're available in stores...and they love their *Heart to Heart* subscriber newsletter featuring author news, horoscopes, recipes, book reviews and much more!
5. We hope that after receiving your free books you'll want to remain a subscriber. But the choice is yours—to continue or cancel, any time at all! So why not take us up on our invitation, with no risk of any kind. You'll be glad you did!

Visit us online at

www.eHarlequin.com

◆ Exciting Harlequin® romance books— FREE!
◆ Plus an exciting mystery gift—FREE!
◆ No cost! No obligation to buy!

◆ DETACH AND MAIL CARD TODAY! ◆

The Harlequin Reader Service®—Here's how it works:

Accepting your 2 free books and gift places you under no obligation to buy anything. You may keep the books and gift and return the shipping statement marked "cancel." If you do not cancel, about a month later we'll send you 4 additional books and bill you just $3.80 each in the U.S., or $4.21 each in Canada, plus 25¢ shipping & handling per book and applicable taxes if any.* That's the complete price and — compared to cover prices of $4.50 each in the U.S. and $5.25 each in Canada — it's quite a bargain! You may cancel at any time, but if you choose to continue, every month we'll send you 4 more books, which you may either purchase at the discount price or return to us and cancel your subscription.

*Terms and prices subject to change without notice. Sales tax applicable in N.Y. Canadian residents will be charged applicable provincial taxes and GST.

If offer card is missing write to: Harlequin Reader Service, 3010 Walden Ave., P.O. Box 1867, Buffalo, NY 14240-1867

BUSINESS REPLY MAIL
FIRST-CLASS MAIL   PERMIT NO. 717-003   BUFFALO, NY

POSTAGE WILL BE PAID BY ADDRESSEE

HARLEQUIN READER SERVICE
3010 WALDEN AVE
PO BOX 1867
BUFFALO NY 14240-9952

NO POSTAGE
NECESSARY
IF MAILED
IN THE
UNITED STATES

frown turned to an all-out scowl when Tag rolled down the window. His eyes were hidden behind mirrored sunglasses, his shoulders straining his uniform shirt. Not that she'd admit it to him, but she knew him now, and could read his tension. What had gotten his panties all ruffled?

"Ready?" he asked.

Ready. Maybe that explained the odd tremble in her limbs at the sight of him. "Has hell frozen over?"

His jaw tightened. "You want to be nice to me today, Cassie. I'm in a mood."

"Oh, fine, you're in a mood. Well, just take it on down the road."

"Get in."

"What's the matter? Am I disturbing the peace?"

"Yeah. Mine."

"Kate is going to meet me."

"The arrangements have been changed."

She was going to kill Kate at the first opportunity. "I'd rather walk."

"It's thirty miles and it's going to be dark in five minutes." He sighed. "Let's go."

She would never in a million years be able to explain to anyone, much less herself, why she stood up and got in the squad car.

Without glancing at her again, he put the car in drive and took off. Cassie looked around her with morbid curiosity. "I've never been in one of these before."

"Uh-huh."

She hadn't, but at his sarcastic "Uh-huh" she folded her arms and stared straight ahead. Why had she said that? Why had she just opened her mouth and let something personal like that fly out? She never did that, and she never would again, or she'd cut out her own tongue.

Another rough sigh punctured the air, and his hand went to her thigh. She tensed, but all he did was gently squeeze her. "I'm sorry," he said. "That was uncalled for."

She tossed his hand off her leg. "Whatever."

With a soft oath beneath his breath, he exited the freeway, took a few turns, obviously knowing where he was heading despite the dark, dark night and the fact that there were no streetlights. They ended up on the east side of the lake.

"What are we doing?" she asked.

"Talking."

She stared into his sharp, knowing eyes. "About?"

"You shouldn't have gone to New York this weekend."

"I was in and out. Never saw Pete. He never saw me."

"How can you be sure?"

"I'm sure. Look, he's probably already lost interest."

He shook his head. "It was still foolish. Foolish, dangerous and *stupid.*"

She crossed her arms. "Well, why don't you just tell me how you really feel?"

"Why did you do it?"

"I needed to get away."

"From me?" He seemed too big for the car. His shoulders and chest and arms filled her vision. So did his badge.

She turned and stared out the windshield. "Awfully conceited, aren't you?"

"When are you going to tell me why you're so bitchy when I'm in my uniform?"

"Um, because it's a terrible color on you?"

"Goddamn it, can't you just answer a question?"

She expertly flipped the deck of cards between her fingers. "Sure, when I feel like it."

He got out of the car, came around for her and opened her door.

Cassie looked out over the black water and felt an urge to strip down and swim off all her tension. "You're on duty."

"I left work when I picked you up."

"I want to be alone. I want to go home."

"We're alone here, this is a secluded spot. Please?" He held out a hand.

She stared at that large, work-roughened hand, at his long, well-shaped fingers. If he'd said anything else, if he'd been a jerk and demanded she get out, if he'd just hauled her out himself, she would have been able to tell him to go to hell in a handbasket.

But he'd said please, in that low, husky voice that could charm a nun. Damn him. "I suppose it's hot enough that I could dip my feet in for a few minutes."

"Good. Bring the cards."

"Why?"

His lips curved slightly but he said nothing as she got out without accepting his help and walked to the empty beach, making sure to walk the walk, to toss her hair, to glance back at him over her shoulder.

Just so he'd remember exactly what he'd turned down the other night. It'd serve him right, she thought, for always so effortlessly making butterflies dance in her belly.

For making her so off balance with just the look in his eyes.

TAG CAUGHT THE WALK. His gaze was pretty much glued to her ass and hips as she swung them all the way down to the water.

He knew she had no plans on letting him get any closer than it took to drive him wild with desire. He understood that, and appreciated the need coursing through him at the sight of her lush body, clad in a hip-hugging, gauzy white skirt and matching sleeveless blouse that was tied beneath her breasts, exposing a good hand span of her midsection.

Added to that dazzling effect was the fact the material gave off the impression of being sheer, that with every movement he was catching peekaboo hints of the soft flesh beneath.

Hell yeah, he wanted her. Badly. But something had happened to him that night she'd accused him of being like every other guy on the planet. Oh, he wanted the sex. He wanted the sex with her. And yet, surprisingly, he wanted more.

And he wanted her to know that. He wanted her to face it, to accept it, because he had the most shocking feeling no one had ever given her more. Ever.

In front of him, she kicked off her shoes and sat on a pile of rocks, watching the water hit the sand. She pulled up her skirt to her knees and leaned back, appearing relaxed and at ease.

Coming up next to her, he took in the gentle rise and fall of her bare stomach as she breathed, and concentrated on matching her calm rhythm. "Remember that night I won that teddy bear for you?"

Still facing the lake, her lips quirked. "I remember."

Hunkering beside her, he studied her beautiful profile. "Do you remember the kiss?"

He was close enough to hear the little catch in her breath as she turned to him. "Is that what you wanted to talk about?"

"No." Sitting, he kicked off his shoes and socks, then took the cards from her hand, shuffled and dealt them each five cards. "Want to play?"

"I'm good," she warned.

"So am I. Poker?"

Her eyes lit with pure trouble. "*Strip* poker?"

"If you'd like."

Her gaze fell to his uniform shirt and she lifted a shoulder noncommittally, but it was enough to decide him. In uniform he made her nervous, not that she'd ever admit it, and he didn't want that barrier between them. "I'd like," he said, and picked up his cards.

"You're going to lose. You'll be buck naked in no time flat, big man."

"If I lose, I'll strip." He lifted his gaze. "And if you lose…"

"I won't lose."

"If you lose…" he repeated, "you have to answer my questions."

"Questions?"

All of which had been met with resistance so far, but he was a patient man. He had this wild, incredible woman alone on the beach with nothing but the water for company, and he was just smart enough to take advantage of it. "You're not afraid of a few questions, are you, Cassie?"

"What about the strip part of the strip poker?"

"If it suits you."

"It's going to suit you." She gestured to her cards. "I'll take two."

"Me, too."

She accepted her cards then fanned them out and showed him a straight. Keeping his gaze locked on hers, he tossed his cards away and peeled off his uniform shirt.

Her eyes flared as his bare chest came into view, and she made no attempt to hide the way she looked him over. "You're in pretty good shape," she murmured. "Considering."

"Considering?"

"Your age."

He barely managed not to sputter. "I'm hardly over the hill at thirty-two."

"Maybe not, but studies *do* prove you are a decade past your prime. But I wouldn't worry too much..." Again her eyes went on a little tour. He wondered if she'd notice he was hard as a rock. "You seem to be holding up. Deal the cards."

Oh, he'd deal. "Holding?" he asked sweetly. He had a full house.

She laughed and slapped down one card. "Hit me once, but don't hold on to your pants, cowboy. It's nearly over for you."

"All talk, Cassie," he said softly, letting out a husky laugh when she shot him a saucy look.

"We already proved I'm not all talk," she reminded him, her voice just as soft. "Or do you need another lesson?"

He dealt her another card and waited while she lifted a sly eyebrow, cocky as hell, so damned beautiful it almost hurt to look at her. "Isn't that something," he murmured.

Distracted with her cards, she didn't look up. "What?"

"You look amazing when you smile for real."

Her smile started to fade and he put a finger to her lips and shook his head. "Don't stop," he whispered. "I'm sorry."

"Don't be sorry," she said, fanning out her cards for him to see. "Just be naked."

She had two pairs. Studying them, he nodded seriously, then exposed his cards.

"Cheater," she said to his full house.

"You know I didn't cheat."

"Yeah. Damn it." A huff escaped her, and she was still shaking her head when she looked into his eyes and brought her fingers up to the knot beneath her breasts. The three buttons came next, leaving the white gauze open but still covering her breasts. "Lucky hand." With a shrug, the material slipped off her shoulders. For a moment she held her hands over her breasts, then dropped them to her lap.

The blouse fell away, and since she wore nothing beneath it but glorious, generous curves, Tag sucked in a careful breath. "You...have to answer a question now."

"I can't believe you're going to stick to that."

"Yeah." Her breasts were white and creamy, standing out in comparison to the rest of her tanned torso. More than anything he wanted to touch. To lean in and nibble. If he kept thinking along those lines, his pants were going to cut off his circulation. "Give me a sec, I'm having a bit of trouble thinking."

Her nipples slowly hardened.

He swallowed hard and forced his gaze above her chin, remembering he'd done this for a reason. "Why do you hate that I'm a cop? Truth."

She looked away. "I'd rather take a dare."

"You going to welsh on me?"

Her eyes flashed hot. "It's no big mystery, really."

"Then tell me."

She wrapped one arm around her bent knees, hunched over—blocking him from the incredible view of her breasts—and started drawing in the sand. "You might remember, I didn't exactly have the most conventional of childhoods."

Not with a mother who'd switched relationships like some switch shoes. Not with an entire town watching, waiting for her to fall on her face. "I remember."

"You might also remember, my mother was—is— fond of men. We had a lot of them around. For the most part, I hated them all. They were weak and malleable. Led around by their egos. Except one. I thought he was different." Her face hardened. "Turns out he was just like all the other penis-carrying humans. On prom night, he..." She closed her eyes. "He proved it. Asshole."

"And he was a cop?"

"Yeah."

God. Prom night... "Weren't you with Biff?"

Her eyes shuttered and he shook his head. "No, don't clam up, I never believed those stories he's so fond of telling."

"Let's just say Biff wasn't the problem that night."

She'd been seventeen. Underage. Tag's gut twisted. "What exactly happened?"

"Probably nothing as bad as you're thinking. Let's just say we disagreed on what I was willing to put out, so to speak."

"Did he hurt you?"

"No."

Not physically at least. "Cassie."

Another shrug. "You know, to be fair to him, I did have quite the reputation. Being a Tremaine and all. It was no big deal."

She'd been a minor, with someone she'd trusted, when trust had not come easy, and that cop had destroyed that trust. Fury bubbled, but she was looking at him with eyes that dared him to offer sympathy. "We going to play or what?"

Reaching out, he stroked her cheek. "I'm sorry, Cassie."

"Water under the bridge."

"No, it's not."

She let out a little laugh. "I know, a shrink would have a field day that I still hate a uniform. Sue me." She grabbed the cards, shuffled and started dealing. "Anyway. End of story."

Hell if it was. "Who was it?"

"That's another question, and…" She looked over her cards. "You'll have to win first. Which I don't plan on letting you do." She showed him her three queens. "What do you have?"

A damn pair of twos. He turned his hand to show her.

"Bummer." Her gaze was glued to his body as he stood up and unzipped his pants. When he kicked them off and tossed them to where his shoes, socks and shirt already lay, she grinned. "I have to give it to you, Sheriff. You're a man of your word."

And that appealed to her, he could see that. With his uniform gone, she'd warmed up toward him, in a way that was warming him up, as well.

She'd sat back, resting her weight on her palms behind her. Beneath the glow of the stars, her bare breasts were offered up like a feast. "You're also a man with the most incredible physique." Leaning over, she ran a hand down his chest, swirled it around his belly button, then toyed with the elastic edging of his dark blue knit boxers.

He was already hard. He knew she was trying to seduce him to deflect more questions, and if she hadn't been so incredibly sexy, it might have been infuriating. As it was, he didn't have enough blood left in his brain to be infuriated. "Cassie—"

"My turn for a question," she said softly, her finger just barely under the edge of his shorts. A fraction of an inch more and she'd meet hard, hot flesh. "Ever been in love, Tag?"

It was the last thing he expected her to ask. And with her finger now dipping into his shorts, he could hardly think. "Twice."

Her eyes flickered. *Disappointment?* "Twice?"

"Kelly May Johnson." Oh, yeah, definitely a flicker. Maybe even more.

Interesting, very, very interesting. Enlightened, he took his own finger on a tour, too; ran it up her arm, watching her nipples pebble tighter. "She was so pretty. Dark hair, heart-shaped face, petite little thing.'' When his fingers ran over one soft shoulder and down her collarbone, she shivered, and slapped his hand away.

''You asked,'' he reminded her, biting back his grin.

''My mistake.''

He brought his finger back to her collarbone and very carefully traced the very top of her breasts. ''I was in fifth grade.'' He laughed when she shot him a look. ''She broke my heart at second recess when she left me for Tommy O'Mara.''

She grinned. ''You were dumped.'' Her grin went shaky when his finger danced down, down…right between her breasts now.

''And the second?'' she asked a bit breathlessly.

He added his other fingers to the one skimming beneath a generous curve over her ribs, his thumb outstretched, just barely caressing the weight of a breast. ''I was engaged a while back. Turns out it wasn't love, just temporary lust. It passed.''

''I've never been in love,'' she said, closing her eyes on a sigh at his caress. The rest of her hand slipped beneath the material of his shorts. ''I've never mistaken lust for love.''

Tag wrapped his hand around her wrist just as she wrapped her fingers around him.

Their gazes met, Tag's admittedly hazy. But he'd just realized something shocking. That no matter what she said, no matter how fierce and cool and wild she acted, she'd never been wanted, craved or needed for anything but the facade she gave people. She'd never been loved for the woman she was on the inside... Cassie Tremaine Montgomery.

Eyes on his, she fisted him. Stroked him. "Oh, yeah," she breathed. "A very nice physique indeed. Are you going to get yours tonight, Tag? Or are you going to just watch me again?"

She wasn't talking making love. She was talking sex. That's how she wanted it, that's all she knew. He understood that now. With sex she could keep it reined in, could control it.

The idea of giving up that tight control terrified her. But she would let go, he was bound and determined about that.

He would show her the way life was supposed to be. That a relationship went two ways. She could give what she wanted, but she would receive, as well. She could allow someone to care for her, even love her. She could share what was on the inside as well as the outside, and she could be safe while doing it.

But then she stroked him again, this time letting her thumb swirl over the very tip of him as she did, and he nearly lost it.

"Good?" she whispered.

He couldn't find his tongue much less use it.

Her other hand dipped into his shorts, too, cupping him, causing him to suck in a hard breath. "Tag? Good?"

"You know it is," he managed.

"I aim to please."

Hmm. She could prove that. Later. But first he had a lot to show her. A whole lot. With a smile, he slid his hands up the backs of her legs to her perfect, edible butt. Gripping a cheek in each palm, he yanked.

With a gasp, she fell flat to her back on the sand. When she went to sit up, he towered over her, still smiling, thrilling to the way she licked her lips a little uncertainly, just before he claimed her mouth with his.

8

WHEN TAG PULLED BACK from her mouth to drag hot, wet, openmouthed kisses down her throat, Cassie watched the stars above his head dance, hardly able to draw a breath.

He continued his exploration, intent but unrushed, which in itself was a new experience for her. Fast, hard, hot sex was pretty much her forte. She had no need, nor yearning, for anything drawn out and complicated. And she especially had no need for morning afters.

Oh, he knew how to use his mouth. And suddenly shortness of breath didn't seem to be her only problem as he worked his way leisurely through her senses, destroying them one by one with terrifying ease.

Somewhere along the way a knot in her belly had developed. It wasn't supposed to be there. This was supposed to be done her way, in her time. "I've… gotta go," she decided, and pushed at him.

Supporting himself on his elbows, still sprawled above her, Tag lifted his head and looked into her eyes. "No more running," he said. "Not from me."

The knot in her belly tightened, but she forced an easy smile. "Surely you don't mean to...here..."

His smile was genuine. And so unsettlingly sexy. "Haven't you ever made love outside before?"

Made love. She swallowed hard. *"Tag—"*

Gently he covered her mouth with his in a kiss that melted her with its sweetness. When he lifted his head, he smiled. "Scared you with that L-word, didn't I?" When she closed her mouth, he cocked his head. "Admit it."

"I'll admit sex is a better term."

"Do you always get your way?"

Now they were bantering, back on familiar ground. She could handle this. "Absolutely. Tag—" Before she could finish, his mouth took hers, and after a moment she forgot what she was going to say. Forgot everything but getting his hands on her again. "Are you going to get to it or what?"

He let out a low laugh, unbearable in its sexiness. "We could." Almost idly, he traced a nipple with the pad of his thumb. She made a small sound, a sound of wanting, desire, and his eyes darkened as he made the motion again. "You're so beautiful, Cassie."

Her heart picked up speed, and was joined by a quickening inside her. The knot in her belly tightened all the more.

Another pass of his thumb over her puckered nipple, and with a low groan, he bent his head, replacing his touch with his tongue.

She nearly died.

She was still trying to recover when he cupped her face in his hands, tipping it up so that she could see nothing but his face, so intent on hers, his eyes shining with promise. He kissed her again, his mouth as firm and hungry as his body, sensual and heated and so deliciously male. Never before had she understood the passion of a kiss, but she was beginning to. It made her knees weak, and she gripped him for support. By the time he lifted his head again, she was dizzy.

"Here." His voice was low, gritty. "Right here."

God knows, there were a million reasons why they shouldn't. And yet, with his hands all over her, with his amazing body on hers, she couldn't remember a single one. "Here," she whispered. "Right here."

The words were barely past her lips before he took her mouth again. Deeper, hotter, then again. And again, yet somehow still leisurely, as if he had all the time in the world. Lowering his head, plumping up her breasts with his hands, he opened his mouth on a pouting nipple, teasing, licking, sucking, and finally nibbling her to a writhing frenzy. Then he turned his mouth to her other side while his hands ran down her body, over her gauzy skirt. "I've been wondering all night what's beneath this," he said hoarsely against her skin.

She opened her mouth twice before she managed to speak. "Why don't you check for yourself?"

With characteristic bluntness, he did just that, then let out a rough groan as he pushed up the material, baring her to her waist. Ran a finger over the edging of her very tiny lace panties. "Pretty." He spread her legs, settling his big body between them. Staring up at her, he dragged the lace aside.

Then bent his head to study what he'd revealed.

Blinking up at the stars, she waited, holding her breath, knowing he was looking at her, open and vulnerable in a way she couldn't remember ever being before. "Did you forget what to do?" she managed to quip. "Because I could—"

He glided a finger over the throbbing spot between her thighs and all words backed up in her throat.

"You could what, Cassie?"

"Um…"

That knowing, talented finger slowly circled, then sank into her before circling again.

Ohmigod. "Uh…"

Another slow, tortuous round of the finger. "You could…use Big Red? Hmm? Your portable vibrator? I don't think so, Cassie. No batteries tonight. Just me."

She didn't miss those batteries one little bit. Arching back, digging her fingers into the sand at her sides, she gritted her teeth to keep from coming. "Are you going to talk all damn night?"

"Maybe," he said with a smile in his voice.

"Just…" She dragged in a breath and spoke through her teeth. "Tell me you have a condom."

"Actually, I have two."

"Thank God," she said fervently.

"But I don't need them yet." He used two fingers now. Around, in, around again, at just the right tempo, as if he knew her body better than she did. He reduced her world to those fingers and the havoc he'd created within her. Oh, yeah, one more time, just one more... but he stopped and dragged a pathetic whimper from her throat.

"Don't worry, you're going to come. Soon as I do what I've been dying to do." He slid off her panties. Used his fingers to spread her open to him. "I'm going to taste you now, Cassie," he whispered against her, and made good on his promise, using his tongue, his lips, his teeth, until she had to bite her lip to keep from screaming.

Then he dragged the most sensitive patch of skin on her entire body into his mouth and suckled her.

She exploded on the spot.

After what might have been a minute, or maybe a year, she blinked the stars above into focus. Managed to lift her head to find him resting his on her belly, watching her closely.

He smiled. "Hey."

"Condom," she demanded.

He laughed and surged up to his knees, pulling one out of the pocket of his pants.

Pushing him to the sand, she grabbed the packet from him and opened it with her teeth. Spitting out the foil corner, she concentrated on her task, sucking in a breath at the feel of him, all hard, velvety steel in her hands. "Mmm, much better than Big Red."

"Cassie," he said in a voice that sounded a little strangled, and she looked into his face. His jaw was tight, his eyes hot, and as she watched, slowly stroking him, he let his head fall back on his shoulders and groaned.

Oh, yeah, power was good, she thought greedily. Bending over him, letting her hair fall across his heated flesh, she kissed the very tip of his penis, eliciting another tortured groan from his lips. Suddenly she found the value of taking her time, and she smiled as she slowly, slowly, rolled the condom down his length.

"You know exactly how badly you're killing me, right?"

"Uh-huh."

Tag, being who he was, managed to let out a tight smile. "I'll get you back for this."

"Promises, promises." Finished, she sat back and let her hands skim over her own body. "Come inside me."

All humor faded from Tag's expression to be replaced with a sheer heat and need that made her tremble anew. Running his hands up her thighs, he held them open, made a place for himself between them, and thrust home.

She cried out, she couldn't help it. She'd never felt so heated, so high, so filled. One stroke and she nearly came. Two strokes, and she did, with another helpless cry as her body became one endless wave of exalted bliss while he continued to move. Then she heard the rough groan torn from Tag as he came, too, and realized he was trembling, breathing as harshly as she was.

Well, she'd wanted fast, she'd wanted reckless. She'd wanted it over so she could get on with her life.

Only as she blinked the stars above her into focus, as she felt Tag's warm, strong arms surround her, as she felt his mouth nuzzle at the spot beneath her ear, she thought maybe the joke was on her.

Because she didn't feel finished with him yet. The thought made her shiver.

With a sigh, Tag got up.

"What—" The words ended on a gasp as he scooped her into his arms.

"I want a bed," he said, then looked down into her eyes. "With you in it."

"Do I have a choice?"

"Sure. Yours or mine."

SHE CHOSE HERS. It was a matter of control, and in her own space, she thought she had it.

A mistake, a crucial one. Because she was beginning to understand that with Tag, control was up for grabs. She didn't like it, would strategize about it in depth.

Later.

God, he had a mouth. A beautiful, glorious mouth that she couldn't get enough of. It would be humiliating, if he didn't apparently feel the same way. The drive to her house was punctuated by fumbling hands trying to feel more flesh. Stolen kisses. By the time they got there, they stumbled out of the car and made it just inside before he backed her up against the front door.

"Here?" she whispered breathlessly.

"Maybe. Yes." He sucked her lower lip into his mouth. "I can't get enough of you." In the next instant he deepened the kiss, sliding his tongue along hers as he rocked his hips to match her needy thrusts. "It's only been twenty minutes, how can I want you again like this?"

"It's crazy," she agreed, her mouth busy taking tiny bites out of his neck. "We should just stop." Only half kidding, she pulled back. "Just walk away."

"Hell, no." His voice was rough. So were his hands as he ran them up her arms, holding them over her head against the door. "You want me. Say it."

"I never say it."

His eyes glittered as he ran one hand down her body, skimming his fingers beneath the lace of her panties. And found her drenched. "You want me. Your body is saying it for you."

Before she knew it he had her panties off and his pants open. Getting the last condom on was trickier, but he managed just fine. And then he was sinking into her wet heat, making the breath sob in her throat as he filled her as no one else ever had. "Tag…"

"Wrap your legs around my waist. Yeah…there…

there, like that.'' Using the door as leverage, he started to move inside her.

Cassie could have sworn she saw stars again as he thrust into her. She couldn't understand the way she needed him more than her next breath, but she did. When he lifted his head to kiss her again, mating with her mouth the way he was with her body, she started to shudder. Within seconds he matched her, barely holding them upright as he found his own release.

"Damn," he finally breathed, and put his mouth to her throat, nuzzling gently. "You okay?"

She realized she was clinging to him, still humming, still pulsing, and not ready to let go. That horrified her enough to force herself to do exactly that.

Slowly, almost reluctantly, she thought, he let her slide down his body until her feet touched the floor. "I guess there's no need to show you to my bed," she quipped, turning away.

With a hand on her arm, he pulled her back, looked deep into her eyes, making her shiver, making her thighs quiver, making the knot tighten in her belly. "Guess again."

MUCH, MUCH LATER, Tag opened his eyes and stared up at himself in the mirror above Cassie's bed. Flat on his back, he had Cassie facedown, sprawled over the top of him. He had a fistful of her very nice ass in one hand, the other stroking her hair.

Next to the bed, on the floor, was the teddy bear he'd won for her at the carnival.

She'd kept it. He wasn't sure what that meant or why it made him want her again.

But moving seemed impossible. His bones had liquefied since they'd spent the past hour tasting every square inch of each other's bodies. "I consider myself pretty contemporary," he said, watching his hands dance over Cassie's gorgeous body. "But that mirror is rather...startling."

She sat straight up and looked at him from sleepy eyes. "Yeah." She got out of the bed, pointedly looked at the clock, then strode naked across the room to the bathroom and shut the door.

"Gee, Tag, think that was a hint?" he asked his reflection, who smirked.

Oh, definitely, Cassie had gotten what she wanted out of him, and now she was ready for him to go. But was that because she truly was done with him? Or because she was uncomfortable with the intimacy that sleeping over entailed?

With a sigh and a groan, he stood. His legs wobbled with the aftermath of great sex. Staggering a bit, he walked across the room and knocked on the bathroom door. "Cassie? You okay?"

"Why wouldn't I be?"

Well...good question. He himself was feeling pretty damn fine. He leaned against the dresser and pondered this, idly running his gaze over an open book. A diary, it seemed, and before he could stop himself, he read the entry.

1. Drive a fancy car, preferably sunshine-yellow because that's a good color for me.
2. Get the sheriff—somehow, some way, but make it good.
3. Live in the biggest house on Lilac Hill.
4. Open a porn shop—Kate's idea, but it's a good one.
5. Become someone. Note: this should have been number one.

A quick glance at the date explained most of the above—she'd written it ten years ago. Still, far more disturbed than he would have liked to admit, he closed his eyes.

The sound of the book slamming shut had his eyes whipping open again.

"Learn anything?" Cassie asked, still naked. As if she didn't have a care in the world, she strutted that mouthwatering body to the closet, from which she extracted a shocking-pink silk robe and covered herself.

"You've just about got your list handled," he noted, casual as she. "And I've got to give it to you, the yellow car is most definitely a good color for you."

"And let's not forget the house on Lilac Hill."

"Let's not. Interesting goals. But it's the second one that intrigues me most."

"Ah, yes," she said with a little smile. "'Get the sheriff.'"

"Well, you did that, didn't you?"

She was good, but he knew her now, or he was beginning to, and he imagined he saw a flinch in those eyes.

"Oh, yes," she agreed, cool as she pleased. "I definitely did him."

Wasn't she amusing? "So now what?"

"Well, I don't know about you, but I'm going to sleep pretty good."

"Alone?"

She turned away. "Always."

Always. Didn't surprise him. What did was the hurt he felt. "Don't judge me by all the other men in your life, Cassie."

She crossed her arms and arched a brow so high it vanished into her hair. "Meaning?"

"Meaning we're not all scum."

"I don't think you're scum."

"But you don't think I'm good enough to share yourself with."

"I shared."

"Your body," he agreed. "There's more."

"No."

"You know, if you keep harboring your emotions like a miser, it's going to be a lonely life."

"Good night, Sheriff."

"That's it? No talking about it?" He heard his own anger and frustration but didn't care.

"No talking about it."

He nodded. Dressed. Walked to the bedroom door.

"Lock up after me." When she didn't respond, he said, *"Cassie."*

"Yeah, fine. I'll lock up after you."

She waited until she heard the front door shut before she went down and bolted it. And only then did she let herself sink into a chair and cover her face.

The damn list. He'd read it, believed she'd slept with him because of it, and the ironic thing was, she'd finally hurt him the way she'd wanted to in the beginning.

But somehow, somewhere, things had changed. She didn't want him hurt, she just wanted him…to not hurt her.

He didn't know the truth, didn't understand, and he never would.

She couldn't tell him.

How could she? How could she explain she'd made that list the night of her prom, when she'd been little more than a frightened teenager, coming home so destroyed, so determined to leave this town and to come back only for revenge?

How could she tell him the catalyst for that entire event had been his own father?

Simple.

She couldn't.

IT WAS A LIFELONG HABIT of Cassie's that when she felt troubled, she went looking for more. Trouble, that is.

Nothing much had changed in that department. By

ten o'clock the next morning she was on the lookout
for a good diversion. Not easy to find in a small town,
but she hadn't been a wild child for nothing.

By noon she'd recruited Kate, who loved her idea
for a ''pre'' show of the store. A private party, much
along the lines of say…a Tupperware party.

Except instead of kitchenware, they'd have it with
naughty lingerie and toys.

Always enthusiastic, Kate came up with a list of
women to invite, which included—among others—
Annie, Daisy and Diane. Cassie came up with…Stacie.
She actually didn't expect Stacie to be interested, but
by the next night, despite the hastily thrown together
party, her neighbor came an hour early, flushed with
excitement, waving her checkbook.

Diane was right behind her, grinning from ear to
ear. ''Hey, babe, let us in.''

''You're…early,'' Cassie said, blocking their way.
She couldn't let them in yet, she had a ton to do.

''We came to help.'' Stacie craned her neck, trying
to see around Cassie. ''Come on, let us in.''

But she wasn't ready. And she didn't need help.
She never needed help. Besides Kate would be here
any second now, and—

''Don't make us beg,'' Stacie said. ''We want to
help.''

''Ah, jeez. Okay.''

''You know, normally Will pales when I go shop-
ping,'' Diane said about her husband as she gently

pushed Cassie aside so they could enter the store. "But I told him I think you're selling naughty stuff and he got all excited. He actually told me to go for broke." The redheaded thirtysomething grinned like a newlywed, making Cassie actually...*yearn?*

That made no sense, she never coveted what other women had, especially when it came to marriage. Being stuck with the same man every night for the rest of her life, cooking his meals, folding his clothes?

No, thank you.

And yet...she couldn't help but wonder. What would it be like to have a man on your side, forever? For a moment she closed her eyes and tried to picture it. The image she came up with was a potbellied man with a cigar hanging out of his mouth and a remote control in his hand as he lay on the sofa shouting out orders for her to follow.

Pass.

Then the image faded and was replaced with the tall, dark, unbearably sexy Tag. No potbelly. No cigar. Nothing but hot eyes and a hot body, and a voice that assured her she was the only woman on the planet.

Ha! As if that would ever happen. Not after the other night, when he'd misunderstood why she'd had sex with him. When she'd let him misunderstand.

"Oh, Cassie..." Stacie grinned as she looked around. "This is wonderful."

"Oh, yeah, it is," Diane said. And before Cassie knew it, all the work was done. In half the time.

It allowed her mind to wander. Right to Tag. She'd been feeling a little raw ever since he'd left her bed, so she'd been careful to keep her car under the speed limit. She hadn't answered her phone. She'd hidden out in the store with the shades drawn while working.

That Tag hadn't found a way past those barriers only made them all the more important.

And now the shop was filling with women. Young, old, in between—including Mrs. Wilkens!—all curious about the famed Kate and Cassie, and even more curious about Bare Essentials.

But it was the oddest thing…from the moment she'd opened the door to Diane and Stacie, to passing out wine and laughing as the women got a charge out of ordering the most outrageous things of their lives, Cassie never felt one ounce of animosity from any of them.

Not a single one.

Was it really possible Pleasantville had urbanized? Accepted change? Grown up? Well, at least some of it had.

"I THINK WE WERE A HIT," Kate said in disbelief hours later as they cleaned up. "Do you have any idea how much money we made tonight?"

Cassie shook her head, still in shock. "They like us, Kate. They really like us."

"Yeah. We're going to make it, aren't we?"

Cassie looked into Kate's eyes and realized her cousin had been just as unsettled about being in town as she herself had been. "A Tremaine woman always lands on her feet. You know that."

"Sometimes it's a long fall first."

"You deserve this, Kate."

"So do you. I love you, Cassie."

Cassie hated getting sentimental, but she'd never been able to refuse Kate. "I love you, too."

And later, when she left the shop long after Kate had, walking slowly to her car lost in thought, she was *still* marveling at the entire evening.

Until a movement in the shadows on the other side of the parking lot made her glance over.

Her heart stopped.

Her everything stopped.

She could have sworn she'd just seen Pete standing there against the building, staring at her from behind the cloud of his cigarette. But that was impossible. She'd called her agent just that morning and had been told Pete was thought to have gone to L.A. and was probably working under an alias.

Still… She quickly slipped into her car, locked the doors, and took off out of the parking lot, craning her neck to see behind her, but she didn't see him again.

Real or Memorex? She had no idea, and though she wasn't the hysterical type, she drove past her house and headed straight toward Kate's. Her cousin would gladly spare a couch, no problem.

Yet she drove past Kate's, too.

And ten minutes later found herself in front of one certain Sheriff Sean Taggart's house.

9

THOUGH IT WAS WELL PAST midnight, Tag heard the car. He had an ear for such things, and even before his mind dispatched the information on the make and model, his body knew.

He had a feeling his body would always know.

She couldn't see him. On the hammock between two trees in the vast acreage of his front yard, his still nearly full beer balanced on his chest, Tag didn't turn his head to look, but just stayed where he was, studying the night passing him by.

Cassie stayed where she was, too, running the Porsche for a long time, and with each moment that passed, Tag just concentrated on the beauty around him.

He wanted her to go away.

He wanted her to find him.

And then she shut off the engine. Got out of her car. He heard the click-clicking of her heels as she sauntered up his walk toward his porch and wondered what she was wearing to go with those heels.

A sexy little sundress designed to destroy his brain cells?

Skintight, hip-hugging jeans riding so low he'd wonder about the laws of gravity?

He wouldn't look. Why torture himself? It wasn't as if she'd let him have her again. Nope, she'd crossed him right off her list and out of her life.

And he was so fine with that. Hell, he had a list of his own. And she was most definitely not even on it. She wasn't sweet, or even especially kind. She would never put his needs first.

She wasn't ever going to love him, not the way he wanted to be loved.

She knocked on his front door. No soft, timid knock for this woman. Despite the late hour and the fact there were no lights on in the house, she rapped her knuckles against the wood with authority.

"What if I'd been sleeping?" he asked lazily, and let out a not-so-nice smile when she shrieked in surprise.

"Tag…you scared me half to death," she breathed, stepping off the porch, probably sinking her heels into his grass as she came toward him. "What are you doing out here?"

"Well, now, that's my question to you." He didn't get up, didn't even look at her, just kept his head tipped back, staring at the night sky.

"Yeah." She let out a breath, and in it he heard everything he'd heard in her voice. Nerves. Loneliness. Fear.

And damn it, it was that last that got to him. With a sigh he left the hammock and took his first good look at her since that late, late night in her bedroom when she'd reminded him why he should have stayed away from her in the first place. She was wearing silky-looking pants that were indeed doing the gravity-defying, hip-hugging thing. A matching blouse with cutouts teased him with glimpses of her skin. She looked like a million bucks, and if he hadn't known about her humble beginnings, he'd never believe it.

But it was the expression she wore that stabbed right through his resentment in a heartbeat. "What's the matter? Something's happened."

"Oh." She lifted a shoulder. "I was just out for a drive."

Uh-huh. "You're scared."

"Are you kidding?" She let out a laugh and lifted her hair off her neck, tipping her head back and closing her eyes. "I just wanted a piece of the night. It seems cooler here at your house. Do you have anything to drink?"

So they were going to play it that way. Fine. He handed her his still-cold beer. Lifting it in a toast, she tipped her head back and drank. Licking her lips, she looked him over, from his bare chest to his loose sweat bottoms, to his bare feet. "Having trouble sleeping?"

Hell, yes. "No."

"Miss me?"

Hell, yes. "No."

"Why, Sheriff, you lie nearly as good as I do."

Setting down the drink, she reached out and ran a finger over his shoulder, down a pec. "Wonder if letting off a little steam might help the both of us."

"Is that what you're doing?" he asked as her finger trailed down his bare belly and toyed with the string of his sweats. "Letting off steam?"

"You have a problem with that?"

His body sure as hell didn't. He'd gone hard at just the sound of her voice. "If that's all it is."

"What else would it be?"

He took another good long look at her. She'd hidden the emotions he'd sensed when she'd first arrived. She was good at that. "I don't know. Maybe you came for...comfort." It'd been just a guess, but he would have sworn she'd flinched.

"I don't need comfort from a man. Never have."

"That's a shame," he said, sucking in a breath when her fingers skimmed up his ribs, danced over a nipple. "You're trying to seduce me."

"Is it working?"

While he pretended to ponder, she glanced at him. Just once, nonchalantly. But it dissipated the sensual haze she always put him in. She *was* scared. She *had* come to him for comfort. He could see right through her, damn it. Did she really think he couldn't?

Whatever she thought, she wanted to keep it to herself. And would try to do so unless he could pry it out of her. "Come inside," he said. She wouldn't talk to him, not now, not yet, not when she was so keyed up.

And hell, he wasn't above letting her blow off steam first, especially if that meant letting her have her way with his body. There were some sacrifices worth the trouble.

Being with her would be one of them.

Silently they entered the dark house. Taking her hand, he led her up the stairs to his bedroom. His bed was huge and unmade, and she walked over to it, dropped her purse to the floor and stared down at his tossed sheets as she unbuttoned her blouse. "I thought of you these past few days," she said.

He nearly did a double take. Had she just...opened up?

"I found myself looking for you as I drove around."

Had she just...said something sweet? Couldn't be. "Probably trying to avoid getting another ticket."

"No." She let the blouse fall to the floor while he soaked up her incredible body. "About that list, Tag...I wrote it a very long time ago."

"I know."

"I didn't even see it again until Kate mailed me my diary a few weeks ago. And while I should admit that after that first ticket, I did briefly fantasize about using you to cross that item off, I never gave it serious thought. I didn't have sex with you because of it." Now she turned and looked at him, the soft truth in her eyes.

And suddenly his throat was thick. She *was* sweet. She *was* kind. "Cassie..."

"I brought you something." In her sheer demibra and silk pants she bent, opened her purse and pulled out a small bottle. "From Bare Essentials. The best body massage oil made." She untied her pants and they puddled at her feet, revealing matching panties. She stepped clear, a vision in sheer lace and high heels. "I've had the stuff in my purse for a week now. I...thought I'd give you a massage."

She was trying to give, in a way he instinctively knew she'd never given to a man before. And while he wanted to demand to know what had scared her, what had caused her to show him a side of her she'd never shown before, he knew better than to push. In her own time, he thought, and moved close. Cupping her jaw, he brought her face up for a kiss that ignited in less than two seconds.

Until she pushed him away. "If you keep that up, you'll miss out on your massage."

"You don't have to—"

"Lie down." She softened. "Please?"

He did as she asked, spreading himself out on his stomach on the bed. He groaned when she straddled him, sliding her long, long legs to his, bending over him so that her breasts teased his back. "Relax now," she whispered into his ear, and then she straightened.

The next thing he felt were her hands, slick with the oil, running over his back, his shoulders, his arms, and he groaned again. Her fingers were magic, alternately strong and soft, digging into his knots, easing them out of his body with attentive care.

When he was the consistency of a wet noodle, she got up. He nearly groaned his protest until he felt her stripping off his bottoms, leaving him bare-butt naked, sprawled on the bed. Then her fingers returned to his body, digging into the muscles of his legs and his feet, then up to his back once again. "Good?"

"Mmm—*hey*—" he yelped when she bit his butt.

"Turn over. I'll do your front."

Oh, yeah, he wanted her to do his front. One area specifically; the area currently digging into his mattress like a steel rod. But first... He kneeled up, grabbed her around the waist and tumbled her down to the bed.

Flat on her back, her body automatically cradling his, she laughed up at him. "We're done with the massage, I take it?"

"We're done with mine." With that, he flipped her over, facedown on the bed. With a smile, he looked at her delicious rear end wriggling as she tried to free herself. Her very sheer panties were riding up, and he took a moment to enjoy the view. "Relax," he whispered into her ear as she'd done to him, letting her feel the length of his body over hers. He lifted up, ran a finger from the back of her neck down her back to the base of her spine, then traced the line of her mouthwatering butt as far as he could. "It's your turn."

"You don't have to—"

"Hush." He stroked the part of her that was already wet for him, just once, and she moaned and arched her hips. So he did it again, outlining her through her panties, keeping up the rhythm she set with her rocking hips. Bending over her, he put his mouth to the very base of her spine and licked her.

With a gasp, she tightened her legs around his hand, as if to make sure he didn't stop. But he had no intentions of stopping, and showed her with his fingers as he continued to stroke in tune with her pumping hips. Faster now, and as he licked and kissed and nibbled his way over a perfect, luscious cheek, she panted and strained, looking so erotic there face-down on the bed he nearly couldn't stand it. He wanted her to come, had to see her come, so he slipped his fingers beneath the panties.

Gripping the sheets in her fists, she whimpered for more. He gave it to her, nudging her over the edge when he sank his fingers into her wet heat.

She came in long shudders.

He'd never seen anything so arousing, and as he slowly brought her down, still stroking her ever so lightly now, still nibbling on her body, he wanted more for her.

When she would have gotten up, or at least turned over, he held her still. "Hold on." Straddling her hips with his legs, he unhooked her bra, letting the straps slip to her sides.

"What are you doing?"

"Giving you a massage."

"But…what about you?"

"You did me already."

"I mean your orgasm."

"Oh, I'll get mine." He poured some oil down the middle of her back, loving the look of it on her skin. "Hasn't anyone ever done this for you?"

"Given me a massage that I haven't paid for?" She buried her face so he couldn't see her expression. "No," she said finally, tenser than he would have liked.

Well, he could fix that. "Come on, relax a little," he coaxed, and ran his fingers down her slim back.

She shivered, but didn't say another word.

"Breathe," he urged when he saw that she was holding her breath. "Come on, deep, long breaths."

Her neck had hard knots that dissipated the last of his frustration at her. Poor baby. What had made her so incredibly tense? The same thing that had driven her here?

Or was it him? He found he didn't like either possibility. Her shoulders were even worse, and he spent long, long moments rubbing her down, firmly, then more gently kneading until the knots were gone. Her skin was so creamy, so silky soft, the pleasure was all his, for he'd wanted his hands on her like this again. As he rubbed and stroked, she was utterly silent, but she was breathing deeply now, slowly, and he could tell she'd decided to relax.

Trust. Had she finally given it over to him? For this moment, at least, and feeling the sweet taste of victory, he got off her, pulled off her panties, and poured more oil into his hands. Then he started on her endless legs. He was a little surprised at how fast she'd given herself over to him, having expected her to protest again by now.

Glad she hadn't, he spend some time on her feet, then made his way up her legs. When he traced his fingers along her perfect and gratifyingly bare bottom, she didn't move. He shifted to her side, pulled the blanket away from her face and...let out a little laugh. He'd done his job all right. He'd relaxed her.

Right into a coma.

CASSIE WOKE with the sun streaming in on her face and sat straight up with a gasp. Looking down at herself, her nightmare was confirmed—she was as naked as the day she'd been born. Scented with her own Bare Essentials oil.

In Tag's bed!

Good God, she'd fallen asleep with his hands on her and had slept the entire night through, as if she didn't have a care in the world.

The bathroom door opened and Tag strolled out, fully dressed for work. Well, if that didn't just top the cake for her. Nope, nothing like a uniform first thing in the morning to rev her gut into gear.

Looking as if he didn't have a damn care in the world, either, he smiled at her. "Hey. Morning. There's food in the fridge. Help yourself, okay?"

Speechless, she could only gape when he leaned in and kissed her cheek, smelling like soap, like man, like an incredibly sexy man.

His gaze ran over her very bare form, heated and flared, but he didn't so much as touch her. "Have a good day."

"You…I…" Shaking her head, she ran her hands over her face.

"Not a morning person, huh?" He tsked in sympathy. "I'll start the coffee on my way out."

He got to the door before she found her tongue. "You let me sleep."

"That's what people do at night, Cassie."

"But…you made me come," she blurted. "I didn't make you come back."

"Hmm." He rubbed his jaw. "I guess you owe me."

"I don't want to owe you!"

He lifted a shoulder. "Okay." With a shake of his head, he went through the door. "I'll make that coffee with double caffeine, okay? Try not to see or to talk to anyone before you drink the entire pot."

While she sputtered, he laughed and shut the bedroom door. A few moments later she heard the front door shut, as well, and then his car started.

He'd left her! He'd left her naked in his bed, without so much as a single sign of his anger about last night. He hadn't even looked disappointed. Or frustrated.

She looked down at her body. It still looked pretty damn fine if she said so herself, so it wasn't that. And it wasn't as if he hadn't been interested. She knew an interested penis when she saw one, thank you very much. He'd looked down at her slick, sleek form and gotten aroused.

So why had he seemed nothing but amused by the entire fiasco?

In her world, she knew men. She understood them. Knew what made them tick. As they weren't a particularly complicated species, it wasn't a difficult task.

But she didn't understand Tag, not one little bit.

She hated that.

TAG COULD LIST about a million things he'd rather be doing on his lunch hour than driving all the way out to see his father.

Actually, the most he could think of was *one.*

Cassie. The look of utter disbelief on her face as he'd left her sputtering and rumpled and heart-wrenchingly confused in his bed had brought quite a few emotions out in him.

He'd wanted to stay in bed with her. Had wanted to wake her in the most interesting and erotic of ways. Had wanted to love her senseless, into that same trusting stupor he'd had her in last night.

And then demand to know what was wrong.

A fantasy, of course. Cassie wasn't ready for that. And truthfully, he wasn't sure if he was, either. To take that step would be to bring them closer than just physically. It would imply some sort of a relationship, an emotionally based one.

His next emotionally based relationship was going

to be permanent, and he still had his specific vision of what his soul mate would be like.

Just because he'd seen a softer, sweeter side of Cassie did not mean she could cut it, and he knew it.

But damn, she was sexy and arousing and beautiful as hell. Good thing he knew that that alone would never be enough for him. Never.

Grimacing, he made the turnoff to the cabin his father had purchased for himself upon his retirement. It was out in the middle of nowhere, on a windy, remote lake with a rutted road, and Tag swore the entire mile-long driveway.

When he got out of the car, the heat sucked the soul right out of him. Or maybe that was the impending visit he'd been commanded to make. He braced himself for the usual stilted conversation over Tag's lackadaisical sheriffing style compared to his father's tight, unbending one. He'd hear once again what a sorry disappointment he was as a son.

"'Bout time," his father grumbled when Tag knocked. "I could have died waiting for you to drive me to the doctor's office."

"What are you talking about?"

"I fell, Sherlock. Now help me into your car."

Tag glanced down where his father gestured and saw his bare foot. Saw the bucket of ice he'd had it in. Saw the swelling and severe discoloration around the ankle and heel.

"I think it's broken."

Tag stared at his father as he moved in to help

support his weight with his own. "Why are you even on it?"

"I had to get the door."

Tag knew he should have felt a wave of sympathy, but he felt only anger. "You mean you waited hours for me to get here instead of calling an ambulance, or better yet, telling me you needed me to hurry? Jesus, Dad." With sheer disbelief, he half carried, half supported his father on their awkward walk to the car. "I can't believe you. How did this happen?"

"I slipped getting out of the boat."

"You could have hit your head."

"I could have drowned. I could have choked on the fish I ate last night, too. It's just an ankle. Now let's see if you can get me to the doctor in a timely fashion."

Tag shook his head and went back for the ice, feeling only slightly chagrined when his father sucked in a harsh breath as he applied it to the injury. "Stubborn to the end, aren't you?"

"How about you? It takes a near fatal accident to get you out here to see me."

"You wouldn't have died. You're too ornery for that."

His father looked proud of that assessment. "How's town?"

"Behaving," Tag said, getting ready for an argument. They always had one when it came to work.

"Then Cassie Tremaine Montgomery must have left."

"Actually, no."

"Humph." His father leaned his head back and, looking a bit pale, closed his eyes. "Christ, was her mother something. She knew how to screw a man and scramble his brains at the same time."

Tag's heart stopped, then started again with an unnaturally heavy beat. "You dated Cassie's mother?"

"Dated? No."

"You...slept with her?"

"Just like every other man in town. But she was so good, I never cared. She had a way, that woman, of making you feel like the only man on earth. Now her daughter, Cassie...born with claws, that one."

Tag's fingers held the steering wheel so tight he was amazed he could steer the car. "What do you mean?"

"Let's just say she wasn't as friendly as her mother."

Tag got off the freeway, pulled into the hospital parking lot, turned off his car and faced his father, all without reaching over and shaking the life right out of him. "It was you."

"It was me what?"

"The night of her prom. You came on to her. In uniform, no less." He fisted his hands on the wheel instead of his father's face. "What did you do, force yourself on her?"

"Hold it right there, goddamn you." His father grabbed the front of Tag's shirt. "I'm no rapist, and no son of mine is going to imply so."

Tag shoved him back then got out of the car, leaning against the hood. God. No wonder Cassie could hardly stand the sight of him in uniform. No wonder she was so reluctant to let him inside her.

But why the hell hadn't she told him the truth?

Back to the trust thing, he supposed, feeling incredibly bone-weary. And sad. So very, very sad. Not for himself, but for one hauntingly beautiful, tough-as-hell, seventeen-year-old Cassie.

"Hey, so maybe I let her get to me a little," his father said behind him, holding on to the open door for support. "She was wearing a dress that… *Lord.* Anyway, she put off vibes that told every man out there she was available, but when you came within five feet of her she burned you. Devil woman to the very core, that one."

Sick, Tag shook his head. Waved to an emergency room attendant.

"Aren't you taking me in?"

The only place Tag wanted to take his father was straight to hell. He came around and looked him right in the eyes. "I want you to listen to me very carefully. Cassie Tremaine Montgomery is back in town. I don't know for how long, but she's here. She's welcome. And if you so much as look at her, I'm going to make you wish you hadn't." He waited to make sure that sank in. All he'd ever wanted from this man was to know he'd made him proud, but even that small scrap of affection had been too much for his father to handle.

And suddenly Tag let go of it. He no longer needed it. He no longer needed anything from his father at all. Knowing that, he turned away.

And figured he'd just learned the one thing that could possibly convince him Cassie would never be able to trust him.

10

AFTER WAKING UP in Tag's bed, Cassie's entire day was slightly off. She ran out of gas. Was rudely stared at by some old biddies at the Rose Café—which reminded her of what Tag had said about this not being Mayberry. She ran out of cat food, and in the grocery store was frowned at by the checkout clerk, then followed to the car by another one, who wanted to know what hours Bare Essentials would be open, because she couldn't wait to get inside and spend money.

Contradictions. Her life was full of them.

In the post office, no one even looked her way, making her quite suddenly realize that not everyone in town was talking about her or staring at her. Which brought her to another shocking thought. Was the entire attitude she sensed here in Pleasantville simply a reflection of her own attitude about the town?

She would have dwelled on that more but had picked up her forwarded mail from the agent and found two more letters from Pete. All of her preoccupation with the inhabitants of Pleasantville flew out the window at this startling reminder that at least one person was dangerously obsessed with her.

At least the return address was Los Angeles, far from Pleasantville, Ohio.

True to form when faced with something that scared her, she refused to think about any of it. She spent the day at Bare Essentials, arranging and rearranging stock on the new shelves and walls, getting more stock delivered by a grinning Daisy, who admitted to wearing crotchless panties—courtesy of Bare Essentials—beneath her uniform. Maybe Daisy wasn't quite as sweet as she appeared to be.

While Cassie and Kate worked, they laughed and talked, and laughed some more, reveling in spending so much time together for the first time since high school. Their laborious efforts seeming a lot more like fun than revenge.

The fun took a downturn when Kate threw her a knowing glance and brought up the subject of Tag.

"You do remember the sheriff, right?" Kate asked, tongue in cheek. She was hanging silk robes according to size on a wooden rack. "The man who's given you three tickets. The man more gorgeous than sin itself. The man who whenever I bring him up you go slightly bipolar?"

"He has that effect on people."

"No, he has that effect on you. And I think you have that effect on him, as well. You going to do something about it?"

"Such as?"

"Such as…I don't know…" Kate opened another

box and pulled out more padded hangers. "At least burn up a box of condoms together."

Cassie, who'd just taken an unfortunate sip of soda, choked.

Kate spun around, then laughed. "You liked that one?"

Cassie wiped her chin. "You never used to say such things. What's come over you?"

"We're talking about *you*. And the sheriff. I guess, judging by your reaction, I should have said *second* box of condoms, huh?"

"Kate. Please." She sniffed, acting insulted because she didn't want to get into this, not when last night was stamped so indelibly in her mind. "We all know I never go back for seconds."

"Yes, but we both know he's different. You're different."

"It's not like that." Scowling, Cassie stared down at the shipment of thigh-high stockings she'd been folding. "I have no idea why we're even wasting our breath talking about it."

Kate put down the hangers and came to Cassie. Took her hands, looked deep into her eyes, which Cassie hated because Kate seemed to see all when it came to her. "We're talking about it because I'm worried about you. I think Pete is a loose cannon, and I like knowing there's someone here who cares about you after I leave. I like knowing you care about him back."

"I don't care about men."

"I know." Kate squeezed her shoulders. "And for the most part, I agree with you. They're scum. But Tag is not, and I think you know it. I think you're scared of that very fact."

"Look, you won't even admit you have a thing for that sexy Jack. You know, the guy who helped you with Flo's furniture. The one you got caught parking with while I was in New York. The two of you are sniffing around each other like crazy. So you tell me who's running scared here."

Kate tightened her lips and went back to hanging silk robes. "I don't know what you're talking about."

"Uh-huh."

Kate placed three more robes in the display, moving very carefully, very purposely, as she always did when she was annoyed. She shot a look at Cassie.

Cassie just lifted a daring brow.

Kate twisted her lips, holding back a smile.

Cassie didn't bother holding hers back, and suddenly they were both laughing. "We're pathetic," Kate said when she could.

"Yeah. But at least we know it."

They left out the deeply personal stuff after that.

And later, when Cassie went home—where she showered and decided to hell with getting dressed again, to hell with anything remotely related to beauty—she tried to relax.

Which is how she ended up on her couch with a half gallon of double-fudge chocolate ice cream and a spoon, wearing a large, shapeless T-shirt over equally large and baggy sweat bottoms, looking like a fashion don't.

Comfort clothes and comfort food were heaven on earth, she thought, shoving in another mouthful as she sat on the couch with the remote, changing channels at the flick of her attention span.

"Meow."

She turned her head when Miss Priss leapt up to the back of the couch and balefully studied the ice-cream container. "I don't share."

"Meow."

Ah, hell. She held out the spoon and watched the cat curl up at her shoulder and very delicately lap at the offering.

A loud rumbling made her jump until she realized it was coming from the cat. For a moment she seriously went still, thinking Miss Priss must be dying from some stomach ailment, but then she realized the cat was...*purring.*

Apparently Miss Priss liked comfort food, too. "Well, what do you know, common ground."

The cat's eyes were closed in ecstasy as she lapped at the spoon, and Cassie actually felt a melting low in her belly at how cute she looked. She dipped the spoon back into the container for more. "Maybe we can coexist after all, huh?"

At the knock on the front door, cat and woman looked at each other. "You expecting company?" Cassie asked. "Because I'm sure the hell not." Reluctantly she set down the ice cream and padded into the foyer. She eyeballed the umbrella stand and one of the long-handled umbrellas in it, thinking that if Pete had somehow found her she could crack him over the head with one. Action plan in place, she looked through the peephole.

Stacie stood there, smiling and waving at her.

Cassie nearly groaned. She was *so* not feeling social. She looked like death warmed over...but then again, Stacie was holding an aluminum-foil-covered plate that looked loaded with incredible calories from heaven itself.

Opening the door, Cassie's gaze locked on that plate, so she didn't anticipate the bone-crunching hug.

"Oh, Cassie." Squeeze, squeeze. "You're here!" Stacie pulled back and offered the plate. "I don't know if you realized but we do a cookie exchange every month—me and Diane and Annie and some others—and everyone is still talking about Bare Essentials. About the party you and Kate gave for all of us. We're just so thrilled with what we purchased, we wanted you to have these goodies as a thank-you."

Cassie, in the act of lifting the foil and eyeballing a meringue cookie, went still. "This is from...everyone?"

"Everyone."

"To me. Cassie Tremaine Montgomery."

Stacie laughed. "The one and only. We sent Kate a plate, as well." Her smile faded a little. "That's okay, isn't it? Because actually, they wanted me to invite you to join our cookie exchange, but we thought you might think it was…well, you know, too small-town. Sort of stupid.''

''I…don't think it's stupid.'' In fact, she could hardly talk. She felt overwhelmed by their openness and generosity. ''And if I wasn't leaving at the end of the summer, I'd join your cookie exchange. If, um, I could cook.''

Stacie grinned and hugged her again. ''If you were staying, I'd show you myself. It's fun.''

''But I'm not staying.''

''I know.''

''I'm leaving soon as fall hits. I have some jobs lined up.''

''You lead such an exciting life,'' she said on a sigh. ''Well…enjoy. Do you have any plans for the night? Maybe a hot date or something to go with that exciting life?''

Cassie looked down at herself and laughed. ''Yeah, hot date. Look at me.''

''I am. You're beautiful.''

''Stacie, I am dressed like a potato sack. I haven't combed my hair or put on any makeup.''

''Really?''

Cassie started to laugh then realized Stacie wasn't. ''Maybe you need glasses.''

Stacie shook her head, looking suddenly sad. ''I mean, I can see you're not dressed for a photo shoot, as you usually are, but my God, most women would kill to like you do right now on their very best day.''

From inside, Cassie's phone rang. Stacie smiled

again. "I'll let you go. Maybe tomorrow we can catch lunch together or something."

"I…" She stared into Stacie's hopeful face and let out a breath. "I'd like that," she said, shocked to mean it.

She thought about that as she went running for the portable phone, which she kept meaning to put back on its base after she used it but hadn't managed yet. By the time she found the thing, under Miss Priss and her big butt, she was breathless. "Hello?"

Dial tone.

Well, damn she hated that. She set it down and told herself she'd just taken too long to get to the phone and whoever had been calling had gotten tired of waiting.

Only no one ever called her but Kate, who would have called her on her cell phone, not Flo's phone. She shook her head to clear it. She was *not* going to get paranoid.

"Meow."

Cassie sank back to the couch, reached for the ice cream and found it nearly gone. Shocked she craned her head and stared at the cat, who had a fudge mustache. "You are a pig."

Miss Priss started the rumble thing again and shifted closer. Then closer still, until she was in Cassie's lap. Only then did she close her eyes and drift off.

Cassie stared down at the big, fat, lazy cat. "You're shedding," she said. "Ugh. Luckily I don't care about these clothes." Leaving the cat in her lap, she reached for the plate Stacie had just brought, feeling a stab of something that felt uncomfortably like a conscience.

Stacie thought they were friends, and Cassie had never said otherwise.

But what kind of a friend took, took, took and didn't give anything in return? *Couldn't* give anything in return?

"I'm leaving in a month," she told Miss Priss. "Stacie knows that. *You* know that."

Miss Priss opened her slitted green eyes and stared at her.

"I *am*," Cassie said firmly, but her fingers sank into the cat's fur. "And you're going to have to find another person to mooch off of."

The doorbell rang again, and Cassie dislodged the fat cat. Grabbing a fistful of white-chocolate macadamia cookies to die for, she walked back into the foyer, figuring Stacie had forgotten something. Maybe she had another high-calorie offering.

She just wished she didn't feel so...vulnerable. Inexplicably, she felt open in a way she didn't usually allow, and for some reason, couldn't seem to close herself off. A little shaky, needing to be alone to regroup, she stuffed a cookie into her mouth and reluctantly opened the door.

Not Stacie.

"Tag," she said around a mouthful.

"Me," he agreed. He was holding up the doorjamb

with his long, rangy body. His legs were casually crossed, his weight on his arm and shoulder, with his sunglasses hanging out the side of his mouth by an earpiece. Then he straightened to his full height, removed the sunglasses from his mouth and used it for his lethal weapon.

A smile.

Only this smile was different than any other one he'd ever given her. This smile didn't quite reach his eyes, and now that she was staring at him so closely, she could see the strain around his mouth, the tension in every muscle so unfairly and perfectly delineated in his damn sheriff's uniform.

And there she stood, holding a fistful of cookies, crumbs down the front of her— Oh, God. Forget the crumbs. Forget that her heart had stopped at just the sight of him. Forget that she could tell something was wrong. She was standing there in baggy, ugly clothes, with her hair piled on top of her head in a ponytail of all things, and not an ounce of makeup on her face.

She felt naked. "This isn't a good time," she said, and started to shut the door on his face.

He simply slapped his hand to the wood and held it open.

"Go away." God, her voice sounded small. She cleared her throat and lifted her chin. "I'm not in the mood for you." She tried to push the door shut but he was still in her way. Refusing to humiliate herself in a battle of the muscles that she couldn't possibly win, she glared at him. "Is there something wrong with your hearing?"

"Not at all." His gaze ran over her face and she wished to God she'd at least put on makeup. Without eyeliner and lipstick at the bare minimum, she knew she looked like death warmed over. And how pathetic was it she still had a grip on a handful of cookies, not to mention the fudge ice cream stain on one breast.

"Cassie, I don't want to force my way in."

"Good. Then go."

"Please. Please let me in."

That low, gravely voice had never failed to knock her knees together and now was no exception. It really ticked her off. "Do I have a choice?"

"You always have a choice, damn it."

She closed her eyes and put her forehead to the wood.

So light she was certain she imagined it, he ran his hand down her hair. "If it's because you're not dressed," he said quietly. "I've seen you like this before."

"Don't remind me." When he reached out and tugged lightly on a wayward strand of hair, she rolled her eyes. "No one sees me without makeup."

"I like you without it. You seem different. Softer. Let me in, Cassie."

"Why?"

"Because we need to talk."

"About last night? I already said I was sorry. I

didn't mean to fall asleep on you, but I don't feel like paying you back right now—"

"Maybe another time," he said very softly, and if she wasn't mistaken, he sounded frustrated, as well, "we'll talk about the fact that you will never, ever owe me for letting me touch you. But right now I want to talk about my father."

Everything within her went still and she slowly lifted her head, thinking she couldn't have heard him correctly. "Who?"

"You know who. My father."

11

"YOU MIGHT HAVE TOLD ME you knew him personally," Tag said to Cassie. "Especially since I asked you."

She lifted a shoulder. He'd thrown her off, just as both Stacie and Miss Priss had. He stood there gazing at her from eyes filled with hurt and pain and anger.

And it made her…ache. Damn it, she didn't want to think about this. She cared about him, she did. But it was just the bottom-line basic kind of care. The way she cared about her dentist. Her personal trainer.

Her gynecologist.

Which didn't explain why she felt the inexplicable need to make him understand her.

"Hey." He stepped closer. "You okay?"

"Of course."

"Cassie." His eyes held so much. "Why didn't you tell me my father was the one to hurt you that night?"

He was putting her on the spot. *No one* put her on the spot. And suddenly she couldn't remember why she'd wanted to spare his feelings. Why it mattered what he thought.

She really needed a moment, to think, to regroup. To build defenses against all these damn strings on her heart. "So I knew him. So I've always known him. So what."

"So, you might have told me. Did you think I wouldn't care? That I wouldn't believe you? That I wouldn't want to kill him?"

This was definitely the last thing Cassie wanted to talk about tonight. She didn't want to hear how he'd found out. She didn't want to know how it affected him. She didn't want to do anything but polish off the last of her ice cream.

Alone.

But Tag was looking at her with an expression of sober fury bordering on fear, and she realized it was all for her. Whether she liked it or not, her past had come back to haunt not only her, but him. "He didn't hurt me, Tag."

"Not physically, but you trusted him."

"I don't trust anyone."

"Because of him."

"That would be flattering him."

"Cassie…" A disparaging sound escaped him. "My father and I aren't close. We tolerate each other at best. You wouldn't be hurting me to admit he should have paid for what happened that night."

"I've forgotten all about it."

"Really? Is that why you're gripping the wood so hard your knuckles are white?"

Thrown off, when she was never thrown off by a

mere man, she turned her back and stalked through the house. Naturally he followed her, because he was a jerk, because he was an a—

"Cassie." He was right behind her, matching her stride for angry stride. "Stop. We have to talk about this."

She whirled on him at that, right there in the hallway. "Talk? About how your father thought I was as wild and fun and man-hungry as my mother? No."

"Cassie—"

"Don't you get it? He knew how I was. Let's face it, Tag, everyone knew, so why should he have been any different? I came to terms with that a long time ago about this place."

"Then why did you come back?"

"Well, there was that little matter of living on Lilac Hill," she said sarcastically. "And let's not forget, I couldn't wait to drive my fancy car downtown just to show everyone."

"You've never mentioned that last thing on your list," he said very quietly.

"It wasn't important."

"On the contrary, I think it's the most important one." He stepped closer, then closer still, so they were breathing each other's air, their bodies just brushing. His hand came up, cupped her face, and his thumb traced her jaw in an aching tenderness that made her eyes burn.

"You wanted to become someone," he said. "You even made a note that it should have been number one on your list. What were you thinking when you wrote that, Cassie? That you didn't matter? You did. That you weren't important? You were. You are.''

"Stop it." She slapped his hand away. "We both know I wrote that list ten years ago. It doesn't mean anything now."

"It does if you don't believe it, that you are someone."

"Oh, yeah, look at me." She lifted her hands and turned full circle, giving him a good look at the au naturel Cassie Tremaine Montgomery. "I'm someone all right."

He shook his head. "My God, you have no idea, do you? How beautiful you are on the inside, or," he said, holding her arms when she would have fled, "on the outside. Cassie, you're just one big fraud."

She struggled, but he held firm. "Don't be ridiculous."

"No, I mean it." He bent a little, to look right into her eyes. "You honestly believe it's the makeup and the body that sets you apart. You know what else? You honestly think the only thing between us is physical."

"It is."

"I don't mind you wearing me out trying to prove that fact, but one of these days you'll have to face the truth. There's more to us than sex." He let go of her arms, holding her with his gaze.

"No." Unable to stand the empathy and compassion in his eyes, she covered hers. "Damn it, you really caught me at a bad time, Tag. Just go away, okay?''

"I can't. I can't seem to stop thinking about you."

Shocked, she dropped her hands and stared at him, then let out a laugh. "That's funny."

"Really? Why?" He snagged her hand, brought it to his mouth. "Because you think about me, too?"

She would have yanked her hand away but he'd opened his mouth on it and was doing something to her finger with his tongue that made her unable to speak. Then he sucked her finger into his mouth.

Her breath caught. "I…I think about a lot of people."

"Me?"

Still watching her, he bit the pad of her finger, just lightly, but she felt it all the way to her toes. "Maybe occasionally."

His tongue swirled over the pad of her finger before working its way to the inside of her wrist. Her tummy danced. Her nipples beaded.

"Do you want me, Cassie? Right this minute, do you want me?"

She forced out a laugh even as she felt her body weeping for him. "Of course not. You barge in here, you—"

"You're such a bad liar."

Her mouth had been getting her into trouble since the day she'd figured out how to use it, and today was no exception. "Okay, you're right," she said sarcastically. "Oh, Tag, I want you. I want you to make love to me. All night long—"

His mouth covered hers in a kiss that stole her breath. "I'm going to pretend you meant that," he said when they came up for air.

"You can pretend all you want," she said, daring him, then remembered…daring Tag was not a good idea.

With a triumphant glare of his eyes, he cupped the back of her head with one hand. The other traced a finger over her throat to right between her breasts. "Not aroused at all?"

"Absolutely not."

"And yet your nipples are begging for attention. *My* attention."

"Maybe I'm cold."

"Ah." Nodding agreeably, he swept his big, warm hands down her back, then beneath the material of her too-large T-shirt, spreading them wide on her bare skin. "Let me warm you then, since you're not aroused at all."

His warm, warm fingers lightly ran up and down, causing a shiver when they just skimmed the very sides of her breasts. "Better?"

"Um…yes." She cleared her throat. "Much better, thank you."

"You're not turned on at all, right?"

"Just still slightly chilled, that's all." But a delicious languid feeling had begun to overcome her, and damn if her hips didn't want to arch to his. Just barely, she managed to contain herself, and bit her lip to keep any moans she might feel the urge to utter to herself.

"What was that?" His mouth lightly brushed her ear, causing another shiver. "Was that a…moan?"

She locked her knees together. "Don't be ridiculous."

He cupped her bottom, then gripped her hips to his so that she could feel how hard he was, and he *was* gloriously hard. His mouth was still doing something mind-boggling to that sensitive spot just beneath her ear and she let her head fall back to give him better access.

"Cassie?"

"Hmm?"

Now his hands slid beneath her sweats, and finding her without anything beneath, he groaned. "Warm yet?"

"Getting there," she murmured, loving the way his fingers cupped and held her butt so that the hardest, neediest part of him was gliding over the softest, neediest part of her.

"But not turned on, right?"

She'd planted her face in his throat so she could smell him better. Realizing she was nuzzling up to him, her eyes flew open. She stared at his tanned, sexy throat. "Uh…no."

He let go of her. Then suddenly her sweats were down around her calves. Before she could grab for them, Tag sank to his knees in front of her. Hands on her hips, he stroked his thumbs over the quivering skin of her belly, then lower. "I'm turned on by you," he said hoarsely, putting his lips to the very top of one thigh. "So turned on I can think of nothing else." Now his thumbs met and together they slid over her mound and slowly, slowly, spread her open to his gaze.

She was drenched.

He looked up into her eyes, his glittering with triumph. "Don't worry, I'm not the kind of man to say I told you so."

"Bastard—" But the word backed up in her throat when he leaned forward and licked her like a lollipop.

"Oh, my…" that was all she managed to get out, sinking her fingers into his hair and holding on tight. It was that or fall.

Then he opened his mouth and took her in with a sucking motion that rocked her world. She couldn't think, she couldn't breathe. She sure as hell couldn't stand, so she crumpled to a boneless heap.

He caught her. They rolled on the carpet like a couple of wrestlers, fighting for space, struggling to remove clothes, biting, kissing, swearing, laughing.

And then he had her flat on her back, arms held over her head. His body, hard and satisfactorily naked, pressed into her. "Still want to fight?"

Slowly she shook her head.

"Want to give me a hint on what you *do* want to do?"

"I saw a condom fall out of your pocket."

He had it on before she could say anything else. She had barely spread her thighs for him when an impossibly powerful thrust sank him inside her to the hilt.

And then she was lost. She was always lost when she was with him, just as, when he stroked them to a simultaneous orgasm in less than five hard strokes, she was found.

How devastating was that?

THEY SPENT the next few nights in the same manner, with Tag attempting to talk to her, Cassie resisting, distracting him with other things—namely her body— and both of them ending up wearing each other out every way but yesterday.

Unfortunately, they couldn't seem to stop. Cassie couldn't seem to stop. The devastating tugs on the strings to her heart just kept getting stronger every single day.

At least she was sure she hadn't seen Pete again, but what she had seen was worse. In the grocery store, no less than four people she recognized but didn't personally know smiled at her. *Smiled.* At the gas station, the mechanic came out and offered to pump her gas—and he didn't want anything for it.

Then she caved and, at Stacie's insistence, went over there for dinner and found her child a messy, sticky delight. She actually got talked into bowling afterwards—*bowling!*—because Stacie had just joined a league. And then, because apparently a weekly bowling night complete with greasy fries and cherry sodas appealed to her in a way she hadn't imagined, she joined the league, too.

Insanity.

Then, when she thought she couldn't get more conflicted, Kate dropped a bomb, saying that already Bare Essentials was such a success that it deserved a chance to become more than a revenge vehicle. She asked Cassie to stay to run it. Permanently. She said Cassie couldn't be a model forever, and she was right. She said Cassie was made for such a thing, and she was right. She said Cassie seemed happier and more content here than she'd ever seen her and…Cassie was deeply afraid to admit that Kate was right yet again.

So why did she feel such an inexplicable weight on her chest? She could hardly breathe because of it. Home alone late one night, she moved through the living room to the den, off of which was a sliding-glass door that led to the surprisingly large, lush, five-acre-long backyard.

There was a lovely wooden deck opening up to that land, on which sat the hot tub that had become her best friend. She needed that friend now as her every muscle was screaming with a tension tighter than she'd felt when she'd been stalked right out of New York.

The water was already hot, and if she'd had any energy left she might have whimpered in gratitude but her head was working on a more important issue.

Her biggest worry of all wasn't the town or the people in it. It wasn't Kate or the store. It wasn't even Pete.

It was Tag.

He wouldn't come tonight—she'd asked him not to. He would want to talk, want to share, want to... well.

She wanted to be with him, but for her, it was all physical. It was, damn it. It had to be, it was all she could give.

But why? cried a very small, very in-the-minority voice in her head. Why did it have to be so shallow, like everything else in her life? Why couldn't it be different? Deeper? More meaningful? *Real.*

Because she didn't know how to do that. She didn't know if she even believed in it.

So physical and shallow it would stay. And while that had been enough for Tag up until now, she was terrified things were changing. She was terrified he wanted more. And if he didn't get more, she was terrified he'd walk away.

At the bare minimum, he wanted to talk about his father. He thought he had to atone for that long-ago night in some way, and of course he didn't.

His father had told him... what, exactly? God, the humiliation of that night hadn't eaten at her in a long time, but it was eating at her now.

She cranked on the jets of the hot tub. Kicked off her sandals. Stared at the water. Had Sheriff Richard Taggart told his son how Cassie had dressed for the prom? What was it he'd said back then… Oh, yes, he'd said she'd dressed like she wanted it.

Had he also told Tag where Biff was heading with her?

And what had Tag really thought about that night?

Why did she care? "I don't," she said out loud, and dropped her pants. Reached for the buttons on her shirt. "I don't care—" But she did, and her voice caught. She cared about all of it. She cared about the store. She cared about the people she'd come to know—Stacie, Daisy, Diane. Damn it, she even cared about the stupid cat.

But mostly she cared about a man she wasn't sure about. With a vicious yank, she pulled off her blouse and stepped into the hot tub, sinking with a hissing breath into the hot bubbling water up to her chin.

Putting her head back on the edge, she stared up at the stars. What if all these feelings were hers alone? What if he was just out for a good time, using her body as she was using his, and after she left he'd happily move on to the next woman?

Oh, God. That thought tore her apart and she put a shaking hand to her mouth. No. No, this couldn't be happening. She couldn't be falling for this place, for the people in it. For Tag.

No. She'd leave, soon as she could. Pack up and go, and if New York still wasn't safe for her, she'd find somewhere else to go, somewhere where there were no strings attached, no—

"Meow." Miss Priss butted her jaw with her stubborn little head.

Which for some reason made Cassie burst into tears.

TAG WORKED LATE, mostly because his head had not been into his paperwork for weeks now and he was helplessly behind.

The extra hours in the quiet station didn't help much. He had too much time to think. And what he was thinking about was crowding around his head, fighting for space.

His father. They hadn't spoken again, and Tag wasn't sure they would.

Then there was Kate, who'd actually called him today to see if he could check on Pete's whereabouts. Tag had been checking daily to no avail. No one had located Pete and he could only hope the L.A. rumor was true.

And then there was one stubborn, ornery, strong-willed, wildly passionate woman he couldn't seem to get enough of. Cassie Tremaine Montgomery. Not his fantasy woman, that was certain, but somehow... better.

She'd asked him not to come to her tonight, and he'd had every intention of keeping himself busy without her. Only there had been something in her voice that had disturbed him, something...lonely. She was hurting, and she was alone.

In spite of all they'd given to each other—and

taken—she was still struggling to keep him at arm's length. She still wanted to separate the physical from the emotional. He'd been all for that, until he'd realized he wanted both. He wanted it all.

And he wanted her to know that.

Tonight.

SHE DIDN'T ANSWER the front door, but since the sunshine-yellow Porsche was blinding Tag from the driveway by moonlight, he knew she was home.

The front door was locked. Good girl, he thought, and walked around the side yard to see if he could find her outside.

The swing out there was empty. But from where he stood he could hear the jets of the hot tub, and continued on that way.

He was caught up thinking about the things they could do to each other in the hot tub, so it took him a moment to assimilate what he was seeing.

Cassie sitting in it. Long, wavy hair piled on top of her head. Bubbles surrounding her gorgeous body, hiding it from view.

And she was quietly sobbing her heart out.

"Cassie." He was there in a heartbeat, kneeling on the deck behind her, reaching for her shoulders. "Cassie. Oh, baby."

She jerked at his touch, whirling around and backing away into the center of the tub while doing so, making him realize with the sound of the jets and her own grief, she hadn't heard him approach.

"You," she said in such a way that told him exactly who was at the center of at least some of this.

"Me," he agreed. "Tell me what's wrong."

She wiped at her face. "What's wrong is you're trouncing on my privacy again."

"Cassie." Knowing she was hurting made his heart hurt. "Come closer."

"No."

"Come out then."

"No."

She was still right there in front of him, but she'd suddenly retreated into herself before his very gaze. He had no idea what was going on in her head. And damn if he wasn't very, very tired of that. "Fine. I'll come in."

"Don't be silly, Sheriff. You'd wrinkle your uniform."

Ah, the uniform. The center of every single argument they'd ever had. Well, he was done with that. Done with all of it. Frustrated, he kicked off his shoes.

She craned her neck and stole a peek, probably hoping he'd left. Her eyes widened when his hands went to his belt. "What are you doing?"

"Getting rid of the brick wall between us." He shoved down his pants. Kicked them away with his shoes. Ripped off his shirt.

And stood there in front of her bare-ass naked. "Not a sheriff right now, am I?"

"It's just a shirt. A pair of pants."

"I know that." He put his foot in and refused to

hiss out a breath at the hot water. "I'm just not sure you do."

"Put your clothes back on."

"Not until you understand."

"Understand what? That you're butting in where you're not wanted?"

"Understand that I'm just a man. A regular man." He sank in to his waist and walked toward her, stopping when they were only a breath apart. "A regular man who's falling in love with you."

12

SHOCKED TO HER VERY CORE, Cassie stared at Tag for one long heartbeat before whirling away. Splashing. Trying to move. Damn the water now, because it slowed her down. She needed out. She needed to run. Not because he was a cop. Not because he'd invaded her space.

But because he'd used the L-word.

Not fair. Definitely foul. Definitely hitting below the belt.

Oh, God. She needed air—

Long, wet, strong arms encircled her from behind. Pulled her back against a warm, bare chest.

"Cassie." His mouth was at her ear, his voice low and anguished. "Don't."

She kept fighting him. And as a woman who'd learned to fight very young, she was good. She was fast. She fought nasty.

"No," he murmured, sliding one arm across her front, the other low on her belly. "Shh."

Shh my ass, she thought, and fought harder, satisfied when water sloshed out of the tub, more satisfied when she elbowed him and heard the "Oomph" of his breath whoosh by her ear. But even as she fought, she felt hyperaware of two things.

One, she was naked.

Two, so was he.

And all that nakedness was rubbing against each other—her back to his chest, her butt to his groin—and her anger was starting to turn into something else entirely, something beyond her control, something…something she no longer wanted to run from.

But there was the principle of the matter, she couldn't forget that. He'd betrayed her by adding all this emotion to the pot. "You shouldn't have said that. That you were…that you might be…"

"Falling in love with you?"

Because she'd stopped fighting, he carefully loosened his hold but didn't take his hands off her. They were standing in the middle of the tub, her back to his front, the bubbling water lapping at their hips. She became very conscious of the fact that her breasts were plumped up by his arm, that his other arm lay across the front of her so that his hand rested across the very top of her thighs.

"I didn't say it to hurt you." His arms tightened, as if in a hug. "It's just the truth and I wanted to share it with you."

She stared down at his big, tanned hand spread wide on her softer, whiter skin and recognized that by just his touching her, she felt very female, very special.

Damn him. "Sharing is overrated."

"Yeah, you're right, it can be overrated. With the wrong person, that is." Slowly he turned her around in his arms. Let her look into his face, where she could see the hurt she'd put there.

Her gut pinched. He'd given her so much, whether she wanted to admit it or not. She wasn't that selfish that she couldn't give him something back, just a little something. "I don't care that you're sheriff," she whispered.

"Okay. Define 'don't care.'"

"I mean I'm getting used to seeing you in the uniform, okay? I'm getting used to it even if it means I can't drive my car as fast. And..."

"And..."

"And...I guess I should say, I know you're the same with or without the stupid badge."

"Ah." His mouth lowered to within a fraction of hers. "Are you sure about that?"

Her breath caught when his body slid against hers. Lord, he had such a beautiful, hard, sinewy, tough body. "Um..."

"Maybe we should make sure. Tell me, for example, do I kiss the same with or without the uniform?" He put his mouth to hers, ripping a helplessly hungry sound from her throat.

At that, he deepened the kiss, dancing his tongue to hers in a way that made her dig her fingers into his arms and press even closer to the body she couldn't seem to get enough of. Obligingly, he leaned into her as the kiss spun out of control, leaned and leaned until suddenly they both fell back into one of the double seats of the hot tub, splashing water, laughing a little, but diving right back into the kiss.

Breaking off for air, Tag put his wet mouth to her ear and slowly exhaled, making her shiver. Making her want more. Now.

"Cassie."

"Yeah." A fog of sexual arousal had descended over her vision.

"Is it the same?"

She sighed. "Fine. Yes, you kiss me stupid with or without the uniform. Tag…tell me you have a condom in those pants on the grass over there."

He slowly shook his head, his thumb tracing her lower lip. "I do, but we're not going to have sex."

She stared at him, feeling a little befuddled. She looked at the hair lightly decorating his muscular chest. At the line of that same hair that divided his hard stomach and vanished with the rest of his good parts into the swirling water. Then she watched his tongue slick over his wet lower lip. Oh, God, she wanted him. Wanted him to obliterate all the emotional tension and get right to the physical. "We're not going to do it in here?"

"No." Leaning forward, he put his mouth to her throat and sucked.

Her head thunked back against the edge. "But…" The backs of his fingers brushed over her right breast as he reached up to touch her cheek. But she wanted his fingers back on her breasts. Wanted that so badly she was shaking. "Why not?"

His eyes were all over her, and their hot intensity as he stared at her told he did want her very much, so she could forget the sudden fear that he didn't.

"I want more than sex, Cassie. I want more, and I want it with you."

Her eyes widened, because…oh, God, if he used the L-word again right now—which would be the equivalent to an icy bucket of water being dumped on her hot, hot body—she was going to slug him.

Then probably start bawling again.

"I want you," he said again through very tight vocal cords. "More than I want my next breath, if you want the truth. I want to make love. Then I want to sit here with you in my arms and talk. I want to know why you were crying. I want to know your hopes and dreams. I want—"

"I get it," she said tightly, bitterly disappointed, and crossed her arms. "But I'm not up for that."

"Really? Or are you just scared?"

Her chin came up. "I am not."

"Prove it," he dared softly, his heart in his throat because this felt as though it was the most important moment of his life. He didn't know when exactly, or the where or the why of it, but this woman had become more important to him than anything or anyone else.

And he wanted to show it to her.

"You want me to prove you don't scare me," she

said to herself, taking a deep breath that brought the very tips of her breasts out of the water. ''Yeah, okay. I can do that.'' Eyes glittering, she climbed out of the water into the equally steamy night.

For a moment she simply looked at him, naked and gleaming by moonlight, and his chest ached just looking at her. Would she go through with it?

But his Cassie was nothing if not the bravest woman he'd ever met, and slowly her lips curved. ''Come here,'' she said in a sultry voice that matched her body. She led him to the long, wide swing, which had a comfortable cotton cover and more pillows than his own bed. Standing in front of it, she twined her arms around his neck, tipped her head and kissed him. Kissed him with her lips, with her tongue, and when she made that helpless sound in the back of her throat again—the sound that assured him she was every bit as lost as he was—he knew she was kissing him with her heart.

His own opened. Flooded. ''That's it,'' he murmured, stroking his hands down her back. ''Oh, yeah, Cassie, that's it. Do you feel it?''

''I feel you. God, Tag, I feel you.'' One of her legs bent, hooked at his hip so that his engorged penis brushed at the very core of her. Her head fell back and she arched closer. ''Please, Tag, please…''

''Oh, yeah.'' He sank with her onto the swing. ''But we have all night.''

''We've had all night before.''

''This is going to be different. More.'' He reached

out a reverent finger to the tip of one nipple, lightly circling it, watching it bead up tight beneath his touch until it distended out a good half inch, pouting for more. He shivered and brought his other still-wet hand up, dripping water over her skin. Waiting until a small rivulet ran down her breast to the very tip of the puckered nipple before he leaned in and licked it off.

With a little cry, she arched up and did her best to thrust her entire breast into his mouth. But he simply pulled back and repeated the feathery touch to her other nipple. She let out a little mewl, gripped his hair in her fists and held his mouth to her breast.

Tag growled and hauled her into his arms. Her mouth raised to his and he took it, groaning when she used her tongue in a blatant motion that mimicked what she wanted him to do to her. Holding her head, he gentled the kiss, sucking on her bottom lip, licking the corner of her mouth before slowly deepening the connection, making love to her mouth the way he was going to make love to her body.

Panting, she tore free and arched her body toward his. "I'm ready right now."

"Are you?" Holding her gaze, he slid his hands down her body to her hips, and slowly rocked them to his.

"Yes!" Spreading her legs, she managed to get the very tip of him inside her before he gripped her hips with a rough groan. His hands were shaking as he held her still. "Not yet." There was still more. He slid his fingers between her legs and nearly fell to a boneless heap when he felt how hot, how wet she was. It was impossible not to stroke her, not to get caught up in her rhythm.

"Oh, please," she whispered, rocking against him. "Please, Tag."

"Tell me." Laying her back, he looked down into her eyes, at her mouth still wet from his, at the body he wanted to make love to for the rest of his life. He skimmed a hand over her breasts, her stomach, lower. Past her belly button, over her mound so that the tips of his fingers divided slick feminine folds.

Her eyes went opaque and arching up, she cried out.

"You want...this?" His middle finger feathered over her while he took her nipple into his mouth. "Or...this?" He slid that finger inside her now, then added another, while stroking her with his thumb.

"Tag...oh, *Tag*." She couldn't stop saying his name. She couldn't help it, sensations rocked and throbbed and demanded completion. Never in her life had she experienced anything like it. Oh, definitely she'd enjoyed sex, more than maybe she'd like to admit, but always...always, she'd kept her head at all times, even during a climax. And always, she'd been able to walk away.

But right this minute, under his knowing, tortuous administrations and his most amazing fingers, she couldn't keep her head. Couldn't walk away. Could hardly breathe. One desperate mass of flesh, she spread her thighs to take in more of the magic. Her fingers dug into his arms, his chest, wherever she could reach, in an attempt to get a grip, but with his mouth on her breast, his fingers buried in her, his voice echoing in her ears that he was going to make love to her until they couldn't take any more, there was no grip to be found.

"You're so wet," he murmured, his fingers playing in that wetness. "Wet for me."

She couldn't stand it, not the kisses, the erotic words, the careful, knowing strokes. Her muscles started to quiver and she was one heartbeat away from coming when he released her breast with an audible pop and took his fingers away, making her nearly scream.

"Not yet." He came up with a condom and tore it open with his teeth while his fingers stroked her one last time. Her toes curled.

"Don't come yet," he begged, pushing up onto his knees between her legs. For a moment he just stared down at her, with such heat and affection and need she nearly came from that alone.

"You're so sweet," he whispered.

Well, that was a new one, and it shouldn't have caught her breath, burned her eyes. Shouldn't have done anything but infuriate her because he was effortlessly holding her on the very edge as no one had ever dared to before.

Then, with just one finger he lightly circled her

opening, not quite penetrating, bringing back the heat, the need in a flash.

Biting her lip to keep from begging, she arched her hips. His erection bumped just the right spot, and he inhaled sharply, letting her know he was as on the edge every bit as much as she was. The muscles of his arms quivered. His hips pressed forward. His face was tight with need. "Now," he said.

"Finally."

"Let me in, Cassie."

She pulled her knees back, opening herself, more vulnerable with him in this moment than she'd ever been with anyone, her surrender utter and complete. Slowly, so slowly, he pushed into her, his jaw tight, his eyes holding hers as her body closed tightly around him.

At the same time he slid a hand down her belly, put his thumb on her clitoris as he pulled out of her slightly, dragging against her needy flesh, ripping a cry of need out of her as she wrapped her ankles around his waist.

In and out. A stroke of his thumb. In and out again. "Here's the more," he murmured, and thrust inside deep.

She burst right out of herself. Vaguely, she heard his low, wrenching groan as he found his own release, but she couldn't stop shuddering.

Eventually, she became aware of his wonderful, warm weight. Of the night all around them. Of Tag's lips as he pressed them to her neck. It was shocking how her arms tightened, how she clung, wanting to hold on to this moment forever.

But after a moment he pulled away, obviously not feeling the same need. "I'll be right back," he said, and she nodded, telling herself she was relieved.

Get what you need, Flo had always said.

Well, she'd sure as hell gotten what she needed.

And now, she didn't need anything more.

TAG DISPOSED of the condom and came right back out, but found the swing empty.

He turned in a full circle, his heart thudding because, damn it, he knew he shouldn't have left her when she'd been feeling so open, so raw. He'd felt every bit the same, and had wanted to hold on to her forever, but there'd been the little matter of the condom to deal with.

Still, he nearly sagged in relief when he saw her sitting on the edge of the hot tub, her feet in the water, a towel wrapped around her body.

She'd left another one out for him, which he slid around his hips before sinking to the edge right next to her. He hissed when his feet hit the hot water.

She smiled. "Wuss."

"I am not." But because her smile looked so good on her, he smiled back. "So."

"Yeah." She sighed and splashed with her toes. "So. The dreaded 'after.'"

"You're only dreading it because you promised to cuddle and talk."

She looked as if she'd rather face the electric chair and he smiled again. God, he loved her grumpy, beautiful hide. "Here, I'll make it easy..." He spread out his arm and waited for her to move in close.

She stared at him, rolled her eyes and shuffled close, briefly losing her towel and giving him a bonus glimpse of her breasts. "Hmm, nice," he said, reaching in and stroking a nipple before she managed to cover herself back up.

"You just saw it less than two minutes ago." She fit her shoulder beneath him and shocked him by slipping an easy arm around his waist.

"Honey, the thing with men and breasts...we never get tired of them."

She let out a laugh. "That's pretty pathetic. I've always wondered...don't you men ever get over being a slave to your penis?"

"Afraid not."

She was comfortable, relaxed, swinging her feet and still smiling. He hated to ruin that, but he had to know. "Why were you crying?"

For a brief second she went really still, then sighed and sagged just a bit against him. "It's... complicated."

"So? What isn't?"

She shook her head and her hair clung to the stubble of his jaw. Stroking a finger over his skin, she pulled her hair free, then put her fingers back on his face. "That was amazing, you know. On the swing."

He looked into her eyes and spoke the utter truth. "I've never felt anything like it."

For a second she closed hers. "Me, either." Then she opened those fathomless eyes on his and they were damp. "It's going to sound really pitiful to you, a man who's so confident and respected, but…I've been thinking about this place, about the people in my life." She turned to stare into the water and shook her head. "And much as I would have denied this even yesterday, I…"

"You what? What changed before yesterday and today?"

She glanced at him. "It's pretty hard to admit."

"You can tell me. You can tell me anything."

"I know." She scrunched up her eyes. "I want to be liked, okay?"

When he just looked at her, she visibly relaxed. "I, um…I want people around me who care. I want a home." She let out a disparaging sound. "I know, it's so stupid. But the truth is, I'm falling for this ridiculously opulent house. I'm falling for the horribly spoiled cat that came with it. I'm falling for the steady job at Bare Essentials, where I don't have to take off my clothes and deal with grumpy managers and psycho photographers." She peeked at him. "Don't you dare laugh."

"Are you kidding?" He cupped her jaw, made her look at him, which she did so defiantly his heart ached. "Tell me you left something out of that list you're falling for. Like me. Are you falling for me, Cassie?''

Her mouth opened, then carefully closed. She dropped her gaze and pulled back just enough that his hands fell from her. "I hadn't quite taken it that far yet.''

He stared at her profile while that sank in. "I see.''

She winced, kicked at the water. "Tag, I—''

"No. You're being honest.'' He surged to his feet. "And it's late.'' He needed to go before he did something asinine, such as try to talk her into liking him. Now that would be pathetic. "Good night, Cassie.''

He made it to the sliding-glass door before he realized he wore only a towel. Swearing, he dropped it to the ground and turned around, looking for his clothes, and bumped into Cassie who was holding them out for him.

"Thanks.'' He shoved one leg into his pants but because he was wet and frustrated, he nearly killed himself trying to get the other leg in.

"Tag.''

At the soft plea in her voice, he gritted his teeth and looked at her. Ever since he'd known her, her eyes had been filled with intelligence, sharp, biting humor, and not a little cynicism. She'd seen and done it all, and it showed.

Not now. Now all he could see was anguish, and he took a deep breath. "It's okay.''

"I never really gave a shit about anyone before,

Tag. I mean, I love Kate, I love Aunt Edie and I love Flo, but other than that—''

''I know.'' And damn him for being such a jerk, because he did. Reaching out, he stroked her jaw. ''I know.''

''I think about you.'' She put her hand on his wrist and turned her face into his palm, pressing her lips there. ''I can give you that.''

''That's nice. It's really nice. But I want more, Cassie.''

She closed her eyes. Turned away. ''That I can't give you. Not right now.''

''When?''

''I don't know. I need some time.''

''Fine. I'll call you tomorrow.''

''I need more time than that, Tag.''

''Yeah.'' His heart hurt again, damn it. And he had no one to blame but himself. ''Right.''

TAG SPENT THE NEXT DAY in a rare form of frustration. He knew as he patrolled town that he was being particularly hard-assed, giving out tickets left and right, but he didn't much care. And when his cell phone rang, he barked into it. ''What?''

''What's going on today, sweetie?'' asked Annie.

''Why aren't you on dispatch?''

''I am.''

Sighing, he pinched the bridge of his nose. ''Then why aren't you calling me through the radio?''

''Because I wanted to tell you that you're being a

jerk, and I didn't think you wanted me to say that on the radio.'' This was said so cheerfully his head hurt.

"Now I know you're getting laid on a fairly regular basis," she said. "So—"

"What?"

"It's all over the gossip train," she said without apology. "So…what's up? You fall in love or something?"

"And why would that make me a jerk?"

"It makes all men jerks at first, until they get used to it. That's why I'm calling, to tell you it's okay and you'll get used to it. So why don't you just come on back to the station and I'll make you some iced tea."

"I don't need any iced tea," he said through his teeth.

"I think maybe you do. Do yourself and the town a favor, hon. Come on in."

13

BARE ESSENTIALS opened with the hoopla of a cocktail party attended by nearly everyone in town. Kate was ecstatic. Cassie pretended to be.

Oh, she was beyond thrilled that the store had done well, and continued to do so the week following the opening. It had given her summer purpose while she waited out Crazy Pete. But she'd also done it in good part due to her yearning to hurt Pleasantville. She'd done it for revenge.

But where was the revenge exactly? What had happened? Somehow instead of fulfilling her list and making everyone sorry, *she* was the sorry one. Sorry in love with the life she'd made here.

Thinking about that life made her want more of it. Thinking about that life made her smile.

Smile, for God's sake.

But thinking about Tag made that smile fade. What did she feel for him? Hell if she knew, but she sure felt something. She felt it all the time; when she was sleeping, when she was driving—okay, *speeding,* with a half-hopeful glance in the rearview mirror.

Only Tag never pulled her over.

Kate had told her rumors were running rampant in town. Supposedly he'd been sullen and serious, so much so that people thought he'd turned into his father. People wished she'd sleep with him again so he'd cheer up.

Well, big surprise, she thought as she got into her car one morning. She *did* want to sleep with him again, wanted that more than she wanted anything, even her old life back.

Because when it came right down to it, she actually *didn't* want her old life back. How scary was that?

Suddenly she realized she'd stopped in front of the police station. Parked. Gotten out of the car and walked inside.

And asked for the sheriff.

She had no answers for him, had nothing to say at all, she just…wanted to see him. Oh, God, that was stupid, she shouldn't have come—

Before she could turn tail and run, he came out of his office, tall, dark and attitude-ridden.

"Cassie." That was all he said. Just her name in that terrifyingly distant tone.

How could he look so damn calm? Her heart was in her throat, her palms damp. She forced a smile and hoped she looked half as cool as he did. "Hi. I just…"

"Yes?"

"Um…" She'd regressed into the village idiot. Damn him for not helping her. "I wanted to see how you were."

He lifted his hands and shrugged. "I'm fine."

"Yeah." Well, hadn't this been one big, fat mistake? "Okay, good. You're fine. All righty then, I've got work…" She moved to the door, furious and sad and embarrassed and needing to kick her own butt all at the same time. "Goodbye, Tag."

He watched her stalk to her car in leather pants and a see-through blouse that had made his body quiver hopefully.

"She looks like she's got steam coming out of her fine ears," Annie said conversationally from behind him.

Steam? He hadn't been able to get past the flash of hurt he'd seen in her eyes. The hurt he'd put there.

"Why are all men jackasses whenever they're hurting anyway?" Annie asked. "Is it because they need to share the wealth, do you suppose?"

He *was* a jackass. Worse. What the hell had he just done, besides let his pride take over? She'd come to see him, something that spoke volumes, and she deserved much more than his cool "I'm fine" crap. All she'd ever asked of him was to give her time. He hadn't bothered to even try.

Well she deserved that time, and his patience, too, and she was going to get it. Even if it killed him. She was worth the wait, and with a little of that patience, she would come around. Because he was worth it, too.

Or so he hoped.

"You going after her, Romeo?"

"I have an hour left on my shift."

"And then?"

"If I tell you, are you going to broadcast it on the five o'clock news?"

"Of course."

Tag sighed. "Yeah. I'm going after her."

"Let's hope she'll have you, boss. Let's hope she'll have you."

CASSIE TOOK HERSELF to work as if nothing was the matter. She sat on the front counter preparing the receipts for bookkeeping.

Bookkeeping meaning Kate, of course, who, as the entire accounting department, not only had a head for such things, but was also so completely anal she squeaked when she walked.

Cassie worked steadily, refusing to think about the little visit she'd made on the way over here. "Men suck."

Miss Priss, who sat at Cassie's elbow, occasionally batting an important piece of paper to the floor, looked up with what Cassie would have sworn was complete agreement on her feline face.

Then she batted yet another receipt to the floor.

"Stop that." Cassie hopped down to get the piece of paper. "Or I'll put you out and let animal control take you away."

Miss Priss yawned, and Cassie had to laugh, but it faded when suddenly she couldn't imagine her life without the damn fleabag. "So what do you think of

New York, cat? Think we should blow this pop stand? I do,'' she said. "Screw living in fear.''

But the scarier truth was…she didn't really want to go. "Hey, you know what? I'm not letting any man chase me from where I want to be. Not ever again. And you know what else?''

Miss Priss blinked.

"This is where I want to be. So…stay with me? Here? Forever? What do you say—we can be old maids together.''

Another yawn as the cat craned her head and looked at the phone when it rang.

"Baby!''

Cassie pulled the phone away from her ear to stare at it. "Mom?''

"Who else! How's that town treating you?''

"Decently,'' Cassie had to admit. "I thought you were on a cruise. How's the boyfriend?''

"He's been upgraded to the husband. We got married on a Greek island today.''

"What?'' Cassie screeched.

Miss Priss fell off the counter.

Cassie just stared into space. "But…but…''

"I know.'' Flo sighed. "But it's wonderful. Love is wonderful.''

"Mom! How could you? You always told me to get what I could from a man and then walk away!''

"Of course I didn't!''

"Yes, you did. You always told me to get out, to

leave them hanging." If she hadn't said that, then what had she said?

Flo sighed on the other end of the line. "I said you get what you can, honey, and walk away if it suits you. If what you're getting is love though, I'd grab it and hold on tight."

Holy shit, how had Cassie gotten it so wrong all these years? "Mom?"

"Yes?"

"I'm happy for you."

"Thanks, hon. I'm happy for me, too. He's wonderful. You'll have to meet him sometime. Hey, our sailboat is ready. Love you!"

Click.

Cassie stared out the window, lost in thought about her mother's revelation until she realized Stacie had pulled up and was headed toward the doors of the shop. She knocked on the glass, waving and smiling at Cassie who, still in shock, unlocked the door for her. "We're not open yet. I've got another half hour to get an hour's worth of work done."

"That's what I wanted to talk to you about." Stacie moved in uninvited, grabbing the sign taped to the glass as she went. Turning it around, she grinned. "You won't be needing this anymore."

Cassie looked at the Help Wanted sign she and Kate had put in the window. "Why not?"

"Because help has arrived." Stacie tore it in two and, tossing the pieces in the air, she clapped her hands. "My mom said she'd baby-sit for me when

I'm on shift. Oh, Cassie, please say yes. I want to work here, in the coolest store ever, with you.''

Cassie shook her head helplessly, laughing a little in the face of such pure enthusiasm. ''But it's a sales-clerk position. Have you ever—''

''I've worked at Taco Bell, Dr. Bean's office, Far-mer's Insurance and, most recently, the five-and-dime. Plus, I'm a mom, was a wife and therefore also a cook, maid and baby-sitter. Trust me, I can handle this. I can handle anything.''

''Can you handle cleaning up the paper you just dumped on the floor?''

Stacie beamed. ''Yep.''

''Can you then handle sorting the new silk pyjamas that just came in?''

''Double yep.''

''Okay, then.'' Cassie nodded. ''You're hired.''

''Oh, thank you!''

Cassie braced herself but not in time. She was hauled into a bear hug that went on and on and on.

''You're supposed to hug me back,'' Stacie said in her ear.

''Oh. Yeah.'' So Cassie lifted her arms and hugged Stacie back.

''This is nice. You being my friend.'' Stacie pulled back to smile in Cassie's face. ''And maybe someday soon, you'll let me be your friend back.''

Cassie opened her mouth, then shut it. Because wasn't that the cold, hard truth? ''Stacie, I'm—''

''No.'' She shook her head. ''I'm sorry. That was

rude of me. You're not ready to open up and I had no right to say—''

"Yes, you did." Cassie had to marvel at the truth that had just smacked her in the face. "You know, before you got here, I was sitting right there on that counter feeling a little bit sorry for myself. Thinking poor me, I actually like it here, I actually like that stupid cat, I like you, I like this life. Now, it just sounds silly. It's okay to like what I've found here."

Stacie's smile was slow and genuine. "So you like me back?"

Cassie smiled back and felt her heart warm. "Yeah."

"Can I have a raise?"

"Aren't you a riot?"

"I do try. You have some forms for me? I want to make this official."

Cassie moved toward the back office. "I'll have to dig for them. Might take me a few. Just start over there with those boxes on the floor by the second shelving unit. Don't open the front door yet."

"Got it."

Cassie, followed by Miss Priss, walked down the hallway past two disastrous closets she and Kate hadn't gotten to yet, past the bathroom, to the small cubicle they'd claimed as their office. With a sigh she divided a look between Kate's spotless desk to her own cluttered, dusty, overloaded one.

Miss Priss leapt up to Cassie's and plopped her big, fat body down on a pile. Not wanting to admit how much that silly little gesture meant, she said, "One of these days I'm going to get myself organized."

"Really? Will you return my calls and letters then?" came a sardonic male voice she instantly recognized for the shiver it put down her spine.

Pete had found her.

14

CASSIE TURNED to see Pete sprawled in a chair against the wall, looking tall, California-blond and cold as ice. He had her water bottle from her desk in his hand, which he raised in a silent toast. "Well, look at who the cat dragged in," he said. He purposely lifted the water to his lips and, smiling at the lip gloss outline of a mouth on the rim—obviously hers—he put his mouth to that exact spot.

Her heart was beating so hard she was certain Pete could see it, but she smiled and backed into her desk, reaching behind her, patting, searching for the steel, pointed letter opener she knew she had there somewhere.

Instead of cold steel in her fingers, she felt Miss Priss butt her head into her palm.

Useless cat!

Slowly, Pete came to his feet, standing between her and the door. "I still can't believe you hurt me the way you did, tossing our friendship out the window. After all we meant to each other."

"Yeah, being stalked tends to make me a terribly

disloyal friend.'' Okay so she couldn't get to the door, but she could scream.

And yet that would bring Stacie running, she was certain of it. And what if Pete hurt her? Cassie would never be able to live with that, being the cause of something happening to her new and very wonderful friend.

And they *were* friends, the marvel of that could wash over her even now, strengthen her. She was more than just *that* woman here in Pleasantville. She had people around her who cared, making her and this place a unit. She had Kate; she'd always have Kate. And now she had Stacie, too.

And Tag. Even though she'd hurt him, he cared about her, deeply. She took strength from that, felt herself stand tall.

She needed that extra strength because Pete took a step toward her. ''How did you get in?''

''Back door. It was locked, but ajar. Not smart, Cassie.''

Damn, she'd done it again with the stupid door.

''I know you told the police I was stalking you,'' he said. ''That nearly killed me, Cassie. I can't show my face in my own hometown. My career is ruined. You did that to me, and I didn't deserve it.'' With a vicious swipe, he reached out and cleared the credenza of all the stock, boxes and papers carefully stacked there.

In spite of herself, Cassie flinched. ''The police

will come. They'll take you back to New York and prosecute you.''

''Not that I want to disagree with you, but you're wrong. You're alone here. The store is closed and locked. In fact...'' He kicked a stack of boxes and sent them flying before looking back into her face with a definite glee. ''Scream. Scream all you want. No one will hear you, and even if they did, no one will care. Not about you.''

He couldn't know that was her secret weakness. That no one cared. But people *did,* she knew that now, and managed a smile. ''You're the wrong one, Pete.''

''Here's how this is going to work. You're going to come back with me. Tell the police you were mistaken. I won't take no for an answer, Cassie.'' He moved toward her and she sidestepped around the desk, putting herself behind it.

''I'm not going back to New York.'' She wasn't, she knew that now. Oh, she'd go back to model, as long as they'd have her, but this would be her home base. Pleasantville. Bare Essentials. It's what she wanted with all her heart, and if she wasn't about to have the fight of her life, she would have reveled in the sudden epiphany.

Damn it, where was the letter opener? She couldn't see it anywhere, but there was King-Size Kong, the latest, hottest, eighteen-inch-long, five-inch-thick dildo on the market. Kate had ordered it for fun, and hadn't quite yet decided on how to display it. The thing was made of rubber and weighed more than a bowling ball. It even had batteries in it, because Cassie had put them in there to tease Kate about how to stay busy during late-night accounting sessions.

"Are you listening, Cassie?" Like a flash of lightning, Pete leaned across the desk and latched onto her wrist.

Tug-of-warring did no good; the guy was as strong as an ox. And because he was looking at her with a sick hopefulness that said he wanted her to try to fight him, she forced herself to remain calm. "Let go of me."

"I'm not going to ever let go of you again." He lifted his other hand, whether to hit her or to grab her and haul her across the desk she'd never know, because Miss Priss took one look at him towering over her and, with a hiss, swiped him right across the face.

With a howl, Pete dropped to his knees. "My face, my face!"

Cassie hefted the heavy dildo and brought it down on Pete's head.

Just as he crashed to the floor, Tag slammed into the office, looking larger than life and battle ready with his gun out. He took one look at Cassie wielding her weapon, at Pete prone on the floor, and shook his head. "Damn, Cassie."

"Did I kill him?" She came closer, the dildo resting on her shoulder like a baseball bat, ready for another swing.

But he didn't twitch.

"Pete?" She kicked him gingerly in the leg with her toe, and would have bent over him to check for a pulse but Tag stopped her. He'd holstered his gun and had put his hands on her shoulders, making her look at him. "Jesus. I came to talk to you, and Stacie told me she'd heard banging back here and— Are you hurt?"

"Of course not."

Gently he gave her a little shake. "Stop it. You don't have to always be so tough. It's okay to lean on someone once in awhile, damn it."

"You don't want me to lean on you."

"Is that what you think?" His voice had gone a little hoarse as he ran his hands down her arms, linking their fingers. "That I don't want you to lean on me?"

She closed her eyes, a little overcome by all the emotions she'd allowed to swamp her lately—as in the past twenty minutes.

"Cassie?"

"No," she whispered. "I know what you want."

"And that is?"

"Me." That still could make her tremble in amazement and she opened her eyes. "You want me. Not just sex, you want all of me. I'm…getting used to that."

"You are?"

Oh, the things in his voice—the gruff yearning, the hope, the wariness. "Tag, this morning, I realized some things. I realized—"

Pete groaned and Tag backed up a step to put his foot in the middle of his back. "Go on," he said to Cassie.

She looked down at Pete. "Shouldn't you—"

"Tell me."

But Stacie poked her head through the open office door. "I hope it's okay that I let Tag in. I heard the noise and got worried. You wouldn't believe the crowd out here, Cassie. Sheriff, the backup just pulled up outside. I think we should—"

"Cassie?" Kate pushed Stacie aside. "Oh, my God," she whispered, looking at Pete sprawled on the floor, at Tag who was holding him there with a foot in the small of his back. "Oh, my God."

"You already said that," Cassie said.

Two more uniformed officers pushed their way through, followed by Diane and Will and at least half the population of Pleasantville, all of whom tried to fit into the doorway to see what the commotion was all about.

Cassie looked at them and felt none of her usual resentment and anger. They weren't there to see her fail, or to make fun of her behind her back. They were there because they cared, and suddenly she grinned.

"What's so funny?" Kate stepped over Pete. "He could have killed you."

"Nah. I was armed." She lifted the ten-pound dildo from her shoulder and laughed.

Tag frowned and exchanged a worried look with Kate. "Cassie, sweetheart, I think maybe you should sit down.'' He stepped back from Pete and let one of the deputies haul him out of the office. ''Come on.'' He reached for her, but she danced away, far too full of joy to be contained. *''Cassie.''*

Kate said her name then, too, and so did Stacie, but she just whirled around in a circle until she was dizzy, finally collapsing...right in Tag's arms, as he reached out with an oath to catch her.

''Hey, look at that,'' she said, gripping his shirt, putting her face close to his. ''Just where I wanted to be.''

His arms tightened on her. ''I think this is delayed shock. Let's sit down, okay? And—''

''Nope, not delayed shock.'' She cupped his face, and right there in front of everyone in her entire world, she sighed. ''It's called an epiphany, Tag. I came here to get away, but I also came for revenge. It wasn't going to be pretty. But the oddest thing happened.''

''What?'' he whispered.

''You,'' she whispered back. ''And Kate. And Stacie. And everyone else. I came for revenge but got something even better. I got you.'' She raised her voice so everyone could hear. ''I'm not going back to New York. I'm going to stay.''

Kate grinned. ''Yes!''

''Someone's got to keep things hopping.'' Cassie kept her eyes on Tag, who was watching her very carefully, very intently.

''How do you intend to keep things hopping?'' he

asked softly. "More stalkings? Another interesting shop? More tickets?"

"Nope." She swallowed, because this is where it got a little risky. Not that she wasn't above risk, but this was the mother of all risks. "I'm going to marry the sheriff."

Stacie gaped, then laughed.

Kate whooped.

Tag went utterly, utterly still. "You're going to marry me."

"Yep." She held her breath. "Because I'm assuming you still love me."

"My love wasn't the love in question," he pointed out, now holding her with a death grip, as if he was afraid she'd vanish.

"No, it wasn't, was it?" She laughed, then kissed him. "But now, no one's love is in question." She bit her lip. "Right?"

"Is that your way of asking if I still love you?"

"A Tremaine would never ask such a thing."

"Hmm." Tag lifted a doubtful brow, then ruined it by shaking his head, cupping her face and kissing her long and hot and wet. Coming up for air, he put his forehead to hers. "I do love you. I always will."

"That's good." She was shaking. *Shaking.*

"It's your turn, Cassie," Stacie hissed.

"Yeah." She took a deep breath. "Okay. Tag…"

"Yes, that's his name," Kate said impatiently. "Damn it, Cassie, just tell him! You're killing us here."

Tag nodded in agreement. "Killing us."

God, he was adorable. How could a man be so hot, so sexy, so absolutely magnificent, and still be adorable? "I love you, Tag. I always will."

"Well, then." His voice was suspiciously wobbly. "What do you say we kick everyone out of here, and…" Leaning forward he whispered a lovely, very wicked suggestion in her ear involving King-Size Kong Dildo and her desk.

Even more wobbly now, she gestured behind her back for everyone to go, her eyes on Tag's as her heart rate kicked into gear. "Lock the door on your way out," she said to them and, with a grin, reached for Tag.

Epilogue

One Year Later

CASSIE LIFTED her fingers to adjust the blindfold and felt a large, warm hand hold her back.

"Don't touch it."

Despite the warm night, she shivered at the rough whisper. "Then tell me where you're taking me."

"You'll know it soon enough. Nervous, Cassie?"

Her body was tingling in awareness. Not fear, but arousal. "No," she decided, and felt a stroke of work-roughened fingers over her jaw as a reward.

"Almost there," Tag said, and tugged on her hand, making her stumble against him. Taking full advantage of that, his hands molded her body under the guise of supporting her. Her legs trembled—a direct result of his hands dallying on her breasts and between her thighs. Her surrendering sigh was swallowed by his mouth.

Long moments passed until they both came up for air, panting like a pair of hormonal teenagers. Then Tag lifted her, carried her for a moment before setting her down.

On sand.

He pulled off the blindfold. She stood on the beach—*their* beach—by the lake, lit only by the barest of moons.

"Today is exactly one year since you told everyone you were marrying me," he said, tugging her down, laying her back, towering over her as he covered her body with his. Gathering her hands in his, he lifted them over her head and held her still. "But since you haven't done that yet, I thought…"

"You thought…" She was breathless already. And dying for him. She'd have imagined this would have gotten old after one long year together but they still came together every single night as if they couldn't get enough.

She had the feeling she would never be able to get enough.

"I thought it was time," he said. "To set a date."

Her entire body, straining for release only a moment before, jerked with shock.

Taking advantage of her pinned hands, he unbuttoned her sundress until she was bared to him. With a groan, he bent to a breast, worshipped a nipple. "How about Labor Day weekend? I have some time coming—"

"Tag." Unable to think with his mouth on her, she bucked beneath him until he lifted his head. "Tag."

"I know." He kissed her so gently, so tenderly on the mouth it brought tears to her eyes. "It seems silly to need the paper. But I do. I need it, Cassie." He stripped off his shirt, shoved down his jeans. Swept aside her panties.

And entered her. Then went absolutely still as he stared down into her face with so much emotion, her throat closed. "I love you, Cassie. I always dreamed of this, of asking my fantasy woman to be mine forever—"

"Don't tell me I'm your fantasy woman." She gasped when he stroked once, nearly begged for another one. "We…both know I'm not."

"That's what makes this so perfect. You're better than my fantasy woman could ever be." He stroked again and they both let out a helpless hum. "Oh, yeah, so much better."

"Tag…" To make sure he wouldn't stop again, she grabbed his butt and pulled him closer. "Keep going."

"If you say it."

"Tag…"

"Say it."

"Okay." Her eyes nearly drifted shut when he rewarded her with another thrust, but she forced them to stay open. She didn't want to miss this. "I never wanted anyone in my heart, but somehow you wormed your way— Ouch!" She laughed when he bit her lower lip. "Okay, I *let* you in. I wanted you in. I love you. And yes, it's time. I want to be your wife. Marry me, Tag."

"Right now?"

"Yes. But…finish me first!"

His grin was full of both love and wickedness as he rubbed his jaw to hers. "As your heart desires."

"My heart desires!"

Beneath the stars and in tune to the lake's water gently hitting the shores at their feet, he did just that. Gave her everything her heart desired.

*   *   *   *   *

1

"SOME MEN are strictly visual. While women might like being looked at, we're more elemental creatures. Some women like to be…tasted."

Jack Winfield dropped the poster, staring intently at her. "Are you one of them, Kate? Do you like to be…tasted?" He wondered if she'd dare answer. If the color rising in her cheeks was brought about by sexual excitement or simple nervousness.

"Yes, I do," she admitted, her voice husky and thick.

Definitely sexual excitement.

"And you? Do you like to *taste?*" she countered.

Yeah, he *really* did. Right now he wanted to dine on her as if she was an all-you-can-eat buffet and he was a starving man.

Which was exactly the way she wanted it. She, the woman, in complete control. He, the drooling male, at her feet. He wasn't sure how he knew, but there was no doubt Kate Jones liked being the one in charge when it came to sex. Perhaps that's why she'd kissed him the second time today. As if to say, "Okay, the first one was yours. Now, here's what *I've* got."

Two could play this sultry game. He shrugged, noncommittal. "I enjoy input from all my senses, Kate. Taste, of course. Good food. Cold beer. Sea air. Sweet, fragrant skin. The salty flavor of sweat on a woman's thigh after a vigorous workout."

She wobbled on her high-heeled shoes.

"And sight, of course. I think men are focused on the visual because we like to claim things. We like to see what we've claimed. Whether it's a continent, a car, a business contract. Or a beautiful woman in a red silk teddy."

She swallowed hard, then pursed her lips. "Some women don't want to be claimed."

He touched her chin, tilting it up with his index finger until she stared into his eyes. "Some women also *think* they don't want to be kissed by strangers in broad daylight."

She shuddered. *"Touché."*

"I'm a sensory man. I also enjoy subtle smells." He brushed a wisp of hair off her forehead. "Like the lemon scent of your hair, Kate. And sounds. Gentle moans and cries. Not to mention touch. Soft, moist heat against my skin."

Kate leaned back against the table, as if needing it for support. Her breathing deepened; he watched her chest rise and fall and color redden her cheeks.

"Yes, some men are definitely capable of appreciating all their senses." He crossed his arms, leaning next to her against the table, so close their hips brushed. "So, Kate, tell me, a man who knows how to use his mouth. Is that really your *only* requirement?"

She licked her lips. "I suppose there are...other things."

"Other things?"

His fingers? His tongue? His dick, which was so hard he felt as though he was going to shoot off in his pants?

"His..." This time she ran her hand down her body, flattening her palm against her midriff, then lower, to her hip.

"Hands?" he prompted, staring at hers.

She nodded. "And one most important thing of all."

He waited.

"His brain."

Jack grinned but didn't pause for a second. "Did I tell you I graduated with honors from U.C.L.A. and have my masters in architectural design?"

She laughed again. A light, joyous laugh, considering they were having a heavy, sensual conversation about oral sex and other pleasures. He found himself laughing with her.

"I like you," she admitted, her smile making her eyes sparkle. Then she paused. Her smile faded, as if she'd just realized what she'd said and regretted saying it. A look of confusion crossed her face. It was quickly replaced by cool determination. As if tossing down a gauntlet, or trying to shock him into backing off, she tipped up her chin and said, "I mean, it's been a long time since I met a man who made me laugh and made me wet in the same sixty seconds."

Bare Essentials—Revenge has never been *this* good!

Kate Jones and Cassie Montgomery have a few scores to settle with their hometown. When they turn their attentions to the town's tempting first son and the sexy sheriff, temperatures rise and things start getting interesting....

#62 NATURALLY NAUGHTY
by Leslie Kelly

#63 NAUGHTY, BUT NICE
by Jill Shalvis

Don't miss these red-hot, linked stories from Leslie Kelly and Jill Shalvis!

Both books available November 2002
at your favorite retail outlet.

HARLEQUIN®
Makes any time special®

HARLEQUIN® *Blaze*™

From: Erin Thatcher
To: Samantha Tyler;
Tess Norton
Subject: Men To Do

Ladies, I'm talking about a hot fling with
the type of man no girl in her right mind
would settle down with. You know, a man to
do before we say "I do." What do you think?
Couldn't we use an uncomplicated sexfest?
Why let men corner the market on fun when
we girls have the same urges and needs?
I've already picked mine out....

HARLEQUIN®
Makes any time special®

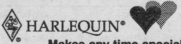